"I'm sorry we have to pull things apart like that, but—" Rich started.

"I know. It's your job." Nicole waved the sheaf of clippings. "This is a tragic story."

"Very." He didn't add that the Ellings' legacy of sorrow—mostly self-inflicted—seemed to be passed from one generation to the next.

"Looks like you decided those old records are of interest." She nodded toward the two boxes he carried and the ones his deputies were loading in the back of the SUV.

"Just taking another long shot." He smiled at her.

She smiled back. Not very wide and a bit ruefully, but the minor thaw sent his pulse trip-hammering. What might a full-blown grin from her do to his insides? As he stowed his boxes in the SUV, he prayed that he never had to arrest her grandmother and rob himself forever of the chance to find out.

Books by Jill Elizabeth Nelson

Love Inspired Suspense

Evidence of Murder
Witness to Murder
Calculated Revenge
Legacy of Lies

JILL ELIZABETH NELSON

writes what she likes to read—faith-based tales of adventure seasoned with romance. By day she operates as housing manager for a seniors' apartment complex. By night she turns into a wild and crazy writer who can hardly wait to jot down all the exciting things her characters are telling her, so she can share them with her readers. More about Jill and her books can be found at www.jillelizabethnelson.com. She and her husband live in rural Minnesota, surrounded by the woods and prairie and their four grown children who have settled nearby.

LEGACY *of* LIES
JILL ELIZABETH NELSON

Steeple
Hill®

Published by Steeple Hill Books™

STEEPLE HILL BOOKS

Steeple
Hill®

Recycling programs
for this product may
not exist in your area.

ISBN-13: 978-0-373-67429-9

LEGACY OF LIES

Copyright © 2010 by Jill Elizabeth Nelson

www.SteepleHill.com

Printed in U.S.A.

A little while, and the wicked will be no more;
Though you look for them, they will not be found.
But the meek will inherit the land
and enjoy great peace.
—*Psalms* 37:10–11

To those who hope steadfastly in the Lord for justice
to prevail and righteousness and truth to reign.

ONE

"Over my dead body!" Nicole Mattson's grandmother whirled away from the stove and planted wire-veined hands on plump hips. "Jan's Sewing Room has sold fabric, patterns and sewing notions for sixty years. I'm not about to toss that heritage out the door to convert to this new-fangled *machine embroidery*." She said the final words with a twist to her lips that suggested she'd tasted something nasty.

Nicole finished shredding lettuce into a bowl and turned from the counter, wiping her hands on a towel. Her gaze met her grandmother's glare. Hopefully, her own eyes contained the winsome mix of firm reason and gentle persuasion she was striving for, rather than the frustration she was trying to hide.

"I'm not saying we should throw all the conventional sewing materials out," she said, "but we need to pare that inventory down and make room for machines that will produce items people will buy in volume. We could market jackets and T-shirts and sweatshirts to schools, businesses, service organizations, churches…" She waved an expansive hand.

Her grandmother sniffed. "But what about the clientele I've built up over a lifetime? They want a quiet place to browse for creative projects—not mindless boilerplate logos and images."

Gritting her teeth, Nicole began chopping fresh vegetables for the salad. Nothing she'd said so far had convinced Grandma Jan that computers and machines could mix with creativity. Maybe the financial approach would work.

"I've studied the shop's books," Nicole said. "J.S.R. hasn't turned a profit in this century." She stopped herself from adding that if the house and shop weren't owned free and clear, and if Grandpa, former president of one of the two banks in town, hadn't left his wife well-fixed, the stubborn woman might be out in the street. "Let the machine embroidery end of the business be my thing. If I'm going to live here, I need to support myself."

A little of the stiffness drained from her grandmother's posture. "Give yourself time to recover from the loss of your husband before you get all caught up in making a living, honey. It's been barely six months since Glen was killed. I remember it took me more than a year to have a clear thought in my head after your grandpa passed. That's why I invited you to come stay with me. We widows need to take care of each other, and the shop will take care of us.

It always has." She went back to tending the meat hissing in her frying pan. "Business will pick up. You'll see. In this economy, more people will think about making their own clothes."

Nicole swallowed a sharp answer. Grandma was living in ancient history if she thought many women were going to add sewing clothes for the family to their hectic schedule, especially when most needed to hold down jobs outside the home. Besides, hand-made clothing wasn't that much cheaper than store-bought anymore. Not that her grandmother would realize such a thing when she continued to sew her own slacks, blouses and dresses. No jeans or T-shirts for Janet Keller, though they were Nicole's favorite garb.

Grandma commenced humming as she added salt to boiling potatoes. Nicole finished the salad, set it on the table and slipped out the back door onto the small deck. The muggy warmth of a summer evening embraced her. The humidity was preferable to the heavy aroma of side pork frying in grease. No wonder Grandma's cholesterol was sky-high. And in the last couple of weeks since Nicole arrived in the little town of Ellington, the woman claimed her granddaughter was too thin and needed plumping up. One more excuse to defy doctor's orders and refuse to change her diet. Nicole grimaced.

Grandma would give a soul in need the shirt off her back—or hand-make them one—but if there was

an award for being set in one's ways, she would win
it. Every change was always "over my dead body."
Nicole ran splayed fingers through thick, dark hair
and released a long sigh.

Her gaze scanned the quiet residential neighborhood in the small town of Ellington. A few of the
1920s bungalows had aged less gracefully than the
Keller home, the oldest house in the neighborhood
and the only towering colonial. Typical of the Kellers
to march to a different drummer, but they paid meticulous care to what they owned. Not that anyone's
property was particularly attractive at the moment.
The paving, curbs and gutters had recently been torn
off the streets to allow replacement of the under-
ground water and sewer pipes, leaving rutted dirt
tracks and, in some places, freshly dug pits instead
of roads. Navigation was a challenge in any direction
from this corner lot. A distant boom echoed. The big
equipment worked on into the evening in another
area of town.

A pervasive sadness sifted through Nicole. Change
happened whether a person planned it or not—and
not always for the good. An image of Glen in his
uniform, flashing his winsome grin, darted past her
mind's eye. She huffed against a stab of pain in her
chest where her heart should be. That organ had
felt cold and dead since the sun-bright winter day
Glen's captain showed up on her doorstep in full-
dress blues, hat in hand.

Melancholy pressed Nicole onto a chair on the deck. When she was growing up and her parents brought her to visit Grandma Jan and Grandpa Frank in this west-central Minnesota town, the lawn was a living carpet of thick grass, thriving plants and lush flowerbeds. Since Grandpa's death a decade ago, when Nicole was twenty-two—a young woman barely wed!—the plants had disappeared one by one, and the flowerbeds had shrunk to a few clumps of petunias here and there. Grandma was not the green thumb in the family, though she'd done her best to maintain Grandpa's beloved rose garden that lined the property along Tenth Street.

At least until this year.

Now the garden looked like some razor-toothed monster had chomped a bite out of it and gouged a trench in the earth up to the house. The gaping hole was part of the city infrastructure project to install new water and sewer lines. Out on the road, the early-evening breeze puffed dust clouds into the air. Across the street, a neighbor emerged from his house, lifted a lazy hand in greeting and ambled toward his garage.

Nicole rose and trod down the three steps onto the grass, then wandered along the edge of the trench until she reached the pitiful remains of Grandpa's beloved roses. A magnificent grandiflora and a prolific white floribunda survived on one side of the gouge in the earth. On the other, several bushes of miniature roses held their blossoms up toward the waning sun. But the trellis with its pink Bourbon climbing roses and most of the hybrid teas, including her grandfather's favorite yellow roses, were gone. This plot of ground had meant so much to him. It was a shame to see it ruined. Maybe when the city project was finished, she could try her hand at restoring the garden. Surely her grandmother wouldn't object to that!

Birdsong teased her ears from a spreading maple tree a few yards behind her. Dappled sunlight reached the trench through the leafy fringes of the tree. As the warm breeze rippled the branches, a pale gleam winked at her from the dirt wall near the bottom of the hole. Nicole bent, hands on knees, and looked closer. Crinkles of dirty white plastic poked out one side wall of the trench. The plastic was at least as wide as her grandmother's antiquated microwave oven, but only about as high as a loaf of bread.

Was this the final resting place of Grandpa's boyhood dog, Lad? Grandpa had, after all, grown up in this house. If so, it was funny he'd never mentioned the beloved mutt was buried here. But it did help explain his obsession with keeping up the rose garden. Then again, that theory could be completely off, and the plastic could contain anything from junk to treasure.

Curiosity nibbled at Nicole. She didn't really care to uncover some old dog bones, but what if it were something more interesting, maybe even valuable. Should she wait until the workers came back tomorrow and ask them to unearth the item? She shook her head. *Nah!* She wouldn't sleep a wink tonight for wondering, so she might as well solve the mystery right now.

Nicole went to the garage and returned with one of her grandfather's gardening trowels. The trench was only a few feet deep, so she hopped in and went to work. A little grunting, sweaty work later she pulled out what turned out to be a package wrapped in a plastic sack—probably a garbage bag. Whatever was inside had some bulk, but was almost as light as air. Probably not a bag of gold then. She smiled at her own absurdity.

The digging machine had caught an edge of the sack and made a rip in the plastic. Standing in the trench, Nicole hooked her finger in the hole and tore the opening wide to expose a bundle of deep blue fabric. A small, faded tag caught her eye. Gingerly, she touched the fragile bit of paper and leaned over the markings. A faint musky smell brushed her nostrils, and her eyes widened. Enough of the letters remained legible to make out the words *Jan's Sewing Room*. Whatever was in here had been wrapped in yard goods from her grandmother's store.

A chill feathered across Nicole's skin. Suddenly, she wasn't so eager to see what was inside. But she was in this too far; she had to look now. Gently,

Nicole rolled the package over and over, releasing layers of fabric. Finally, the contents lay plain to see.

Oxygen fled her lungs. She blinked and stared.

Not a dog. No, not at all.

Someone had buried a *baby* in her grandparents' backyard!

Nicole's head swam, and she gripped the side of the trench, whimpering. Her fingers clawed into the cool earth. Could Grandma Jan have had a miscarriage or a stillbirth? But wouldn't those remains be placed in a cemetery with an official headstone? No whisper of such a family tragedy had reached her ears as she grew up. How about an abortion? Nicole shook her head. These remains were too large for some furtive termination of a rejected pregnancy. This child had probably been at least several months old. And he or she must have been buried here for a long time. Had Grandpa known what precious treasure lay beneath his roses?

What kind of question was that? She shook herself. Of course, Grandpa couldn't have known. He would never have—

"Nicole, I've been calling you to come in for supper. I—" Her grandmother's voice behind her ended in a sharp gasp.

Time suspended like a clock's pendulum gone still.

Nicole finally sucked in a breath, as Grandma Jan let out a shrill cry.

"Oh, no!" The elderly woman's cracked wail held every second of her seventy-five years of existence. "I can't believe it! I never thought… It can't be."

Nicole turned to find her grandmother scuttling away in a half crouch, as if someone had struck her in the stomach, but she must ignore the pain and flee. Grandma was clearly surprised the remains were in her yard, yet she knew something about them. What?

Nicole heaved herself out of the trench and followed, calling for her grandmother to stop. The woman didn't acknowledge that she'd heard. Nicole trailed her through the kitchen and up the hallway. The older woman could move surprisingly fast. Grandma darted into her bedroom, and slammed the door in Nicole's face, barely missing her nose.

Nicole gaped at the closed portal. "What's going on? Whose remains are those?"

"I'm not sure, dear." The thin response carried faintly.

The sound of drawers slamming and the rustling of papers reached Nicole's ears. What was her grandmother looking for?

"I have to call the police." Nicole leaned her forehead against the door panel.

"Do what you need to do, honey. Let me be, now."

On reluctant feet, Nicole went to the kitchen and

lifted the telephone receiver. Why was her grandmother lying to her? And what was she rummaging
for in the bedroom? Something to do with the child
in the rose garden?

Nicole had come to the quiet community of
Ellington—to this home she'd known as a haven
since childhood—in order to rebuild her life after a
devastating loss. More than that, she'd come to look
after her only close living relative in the waning
years of the woman's life. What might happen to
both of them the minute she placed this phone call
to the police station?

Police Chief Rich Hendricks caught the coded
call-out from the dispatcher on his police scanner at
home. He immediately phoned the station for details
not given over the radio, and then abandoned his
half-eaten, fast-food cheeseburger. Small loss. No
fun scarfing down meals alone all the time anyway.
With his wife, Karen, having passed away three years
ago and his daughter, Katrina, newly graduated and
off to summer Bible camp as a counselor, life had
turned pretty blah. A case like this broke up the
routine big-time, but it wasn't the kind of excitement
he welcomed.

A baby's bones found in a trench? When he took
the chief job here in Ellington, he researched the
town, particularly the criminal history. This little
burg hadn't had a mystery this big since Simon

Elling's infant son was kidnapped in 1957 and never recovered. Had the child just been found? And in the Kellers' backyard, no less!

Bouncing over the rough terrain on the dug-up streets, Rich's SUV turned onto Tenth Street. The Keller colonial lay up ahead. Looked as if he was the first unit on the scene, but then, he only lived a few blocks away.

A slender, dark-haired woman stood slump-shouldered beside a bundle on the ground. Nicole Mattson, Jan's granddaughter. She moved to town only a couple of weeks ago, presumably to start a new life a few months after her Minneapolis police-officer husband was killed in a shoot-out with a team of serial bank robbers. The guy was a bonafide hero, decorated and everything, but that didn't make Nicole any less a widow. He sympathized.

Welcome to Ellington.

Rich snorted. This was *not* the way he'd hoped to be introduced to this woman. He'd been eyeing her from afar, giving her space to settle in and time for the sharpest pangs of loss to subside. Since Karen's passing, Nicole was the first female to spark his interest in dating again…and now he had to approach her in cop mode.

He cruised the SUV to the nonexistent curb, grabbed his interview notebook and got out. She gazed at him, brow furrowed above deep brown eyes.

He glanced down at his jeans and Minnesota Vikings T-shirt.

"Sorry." He sent her a muted smile. "This caught me off duty at home. You must be Nicole, Jan's granddaughter. I'm Police Chief Rich Hendricks." He held out his hand.

She took it with a surprisingly firm grip for such a delicate hand and petite frame. Her brown eyes held equal parts sorrow and strength. Nothing squeamish about her, but then she'd been a cop's wife, and her dad, Jan and Frank's son, had been a cop, as well. At least, he wouldn't have to deal with feminine hysterics. He liked her already, though she hadn't said a word.

"This is what I found." She pointed toward the bundle at her feet. "I dug it out of there." She motioned toward a gap in the soil near the bottom of the trench.

Rich narrowed his gaze. The remains hadn't been buried very deep—only about three feet. He made a note in his book, and then squatted beside the dirt-crusted bundle. A plastic object lay on the fabric. He nudged it with the end of his pen, and it rattled. A baby's toy. It looked like the rattle had once been blue and white. The bits of clothing that survived might possibly have been red.

"The remains were wound tightly in the yard goods," Nicole volunteered. "I unwrapped it having no idea I'd find something like *this!*"

Rich nodded her direction. "You did fine. How could you guess?"

Nicole squatted beside him. "What's that?" She pointed to another object in the bundle, partially covered by cloth.

Rich nudged the item into view—a small metal cross. That and the careful shroudlike wrapping sent a message: whoever buried the child either felt remorse or actually cared for the infant.

A tag on the fabric caught his eye. He leaned close and made out the store label. His gaze met Nicole's, but she looked away quickly. Not fast enough to hide the confusion and fear playing across her face. She was afraid her grandmother had something to do with this. A logical conclusion, given the circumstances. He needed to talk to Jan Keller right away.

He rose, Nicole beside him, and swiveled toward the sound of approaching vehicles. A police sedan, followed by the VW Jetta driven by one of their local doctors, pulled up behind his SUV. Rich's lanky deputy, Terry Bender, climbed out of the sedan, cowboy boots first, beneath uniform slacks.

"Bring the yellow tape," Rich called to him. "We'll have to cordon off the area."

The deputy shot him a thumbs-up and ducked back inside his car. Dr. Sharla Mead approached, carrying her kit. The pear-shaped woman around Rich's own age of thirty-nine was the county medical

examiner, as well as chief of staff at the small Ellington hospital.

The doctor gazed down at the bundle and shook
her head. "I'll do my best with COD, but you'll need
a forensics specialist out here to examine the whole
package."

Rich nodded. "Do what you can. Terry will give
you a hand. I'll call someone in from the Minnesota
Bureau of Criminal Apprehension. This kind of case
ought to be right up their alley." Sharla nodded, and
Rich turned toward Nicole. "Is your grandmother
around? We need to visit."

White-faced, Nicole nodded. "She's in the house.
Come with me."

He'd follow her graceful form anywhere, any day,
but interviewing a local senior citizen about a long-
dead infant in her yard was not on his list of fun
things to do, especially with an attractive woman
around. They entered the back door into the kitchen.
Jan Keller was seated at the table with her face in her
hands. A full meal lay before her—meat congealing
in its own grease, mashed potatoes, salad—but the
dinner plates were clean and empty. Not surprising
that no one had an appetite.

Jan looked up, her craggy face set in stone, though
a suspicion of wetness smeared her cheeks. "I know
you've gotta do your duty and ask all sorts of questions, Rich, but you could just as well save your
breath. I can't tell you one thing that will help."

Rich opened his notebook. Did she mean *can't* because she had no idea how the infant ended up buried beneath the rose garden, or *can't* because she *won't* spill what she knows? His gaze bored into hers, and color gradually seeped from her face. Her stare hid fear, or he'd eat his badge.

He groaned inwardly. If Jan Keller had been involved in what could well be the Elling infant's kidnapping and murder, he'd have to arrest a pillar of the community, and she'd spend her waning years in the penitentiary.

His gaze shifted to Nicole, who leaned her back against the counter, arms crossed. The parted lips, pinched nostrils and wide eyes telegraphed desperation. If he took from her life the last bit of family she possessed, he could kiss any dream of romance goodbye.

TWO

Rich stood next to the trench and closed his cell phone, having finished speaking to a liaison at the Minnesota Bureau of Criminal Apprehension. Janet Keller hadn't told him a thing, but maybe the physical evidence would. A forensics tech from the MBCA would be here in the morning. Dr. Mead was transporting the remains to the hospital where they would await the tech's arrival.

"Keep the crime-scene tape up and cover the trench with a tarp," Rich told Terry. "The tech might want to collect soil or check for other evidence from the site."

"Sure thing, Chief." His deputy grinned. "Don't mind hangin' around a little longer. Maybe catch another glimpse of that Keller girl. I remember when this pint-size squirt in pigtails used to visit her grandparents. She sure did grow up into somethin' to look at."

Rich frowned. "I didn't live in Ellington that long

ago, and you must've been a grown man already back then."

"You sayin' I'm too old for her?" The grin faded. "You're not much younger than me, and I can tell you're not immune to the lady's charms."

Rich didn't bother to mention that he was more than half a decade younger than his deputy. The guy already had a hard time accepting him as boss without rubbing in the age difference. "I'm saying you've been in law enforcement too long to let a pretty face distract you."

Terry chuckled, but there was an edge to the sound. "A pretty face doesn't distract me but it always attracts me."

Pressing his lips together, Rich waved to Terry and headed for his SUV. If Nicole fell for Terry's lines, she wasn't the woman he figured her for. Right now, he'd better concentrate on *his* duty. He climbed into his vehicle and checked his watch. Going on 8:00 p.m. But this set of interviews couldn't wait until tomorrow. By then, rumors would be running rampant and catching a fresh reaction would be impossible.

Rich turned his vehicle toward the west and the house on the hill. Perched on the highest bump on this stretch of prairie, the Elling mansion brooded over the town like a disapproving parent. Simon Elling, the current patriarch of the founding family, lived there with his wife and assorted relatives. A sparse and motley crew, far from their heyday as the landed gentry of the county, when Ellings occupied most farmhouses within a thirty-mile radius. But they hadn't lost a bit of their arrogance despite their dwindling numbers. This visit promised to be interesting.

He turned into the driveway that took him toward the circular drive in front of a three-story brick structure that rambled across half an acre of brown-patched lawn. The grass was faintly shaggy and the trees old and balding. The Ellings hadn't employed a yardman in years. He stopped the vehicle near the set of broad stone steps that led to the front doors.

Pressing the doorbell button brought no sound or response from inside, so Rich gave the door sharp raps. Soon a panel swung ajar, and a statuesque woman with a pale, cold face stared out at him. The pulled shape of her gray-blue eyes betrayed one too many face-lifts. He wasn't much of a judge of clothing, but he was pretty certain her silky-looking blouse and form-fitting pants cost more than Daddy would be happy to pay—as soon as he saw the credit-card bill. As far as Rich knew, Simon's fiftysome-thing daughter hadn't worked a day in her life, but she always dressed as if she lived around the corner from a New York boutique.

"Hi, Melody. Is your father in?"

Her artificially plump lips thinned. "What's Mason done now?"

"This isn't about your son."

Her eyes widened. "It's not?"

He didn't blame Melody for being surprised. "I need to talk to Simon regarding a matter that's just come up."

"Can't this wait until tomorrow? The old man's locked himself in his study again." One side of her mouth twisted into a sneer, a typical expression of this thrice-divorced former beauty queen.

"This isn't a social call. It's urgent."

Melody shrugged one shoulder and motioned him inside. "Take your chances, then."

He stepped into an enormous foyer with a vaulted ceiling. The westering sun poured a river of light through the stained glass in the fan window above the doors and sprinkled rainbow colors over a scuffed tile floor. A large Terry Redlin painting hung over an entry table along the wall, but it was a print. If they'd once owned the original, it had been sold long ago. Rich followed Melody's designer-clad form up a hallway, where another pair of double doors confronted him.

"Just give a knock and see what happens." Melody snickered and walked away.

Rich tapped with his knuckles. "Simon. It's Chief Hendricks. I need to talk to you."

Seconds later, a lock rattled and the door flung wide. A tall, sharp-faced man in his late seventies glared out at him. He cradled a brandy snifter a quarter full of dark liquid in one hand. "What's that worthless grandson of mine done now?"

Rich stifled a sigh. "Whatever he's up to, we'll catch him, but this visit isn't about him. The remains of an infant have been found buried in a shallow grave."

"Where?" The snifter froze halfway to Simon's mouth.

"In town."

"A recent burial?"

"Old."

Simon's Adam's apple bobbed. "Come in."

The study sprawled in faded elegance. Spacious dimensions, a long wet bar and a coffered ceiling clamored privilege and power, but thin spots on the carpet and the worn chairs angled toward the cold fireplace betrayed tight times. Simon led the way to a massive mahogany desk and plopped into a leather chair behind it, motioning for his guest to sit in the chair on the other side. Rich remained standing, the better to observe the man at the desk. Simon's free hand gripped the arm of his chair is if he thought it might suddenly buck like a bronco.

"Details," the senior Elling barked.

"Not many yet. The body was buried beneath Janet Keller's rose garden." That much would be common knowledge in less than a day around this small town. He withheld the information that the bones had been wrapped in yard goods from Jan's Sewing Room.

Simon sat up stiff. "You don't suppose Jan or Frank had anything to do with the kidnapping?"

"It's too soon to suppose anything. We don't even know for sure whose remains those bones are. Do you have any reason to think either of the Kellers might have taken your child? Bad blood of any kind? Raw business dealings?"

Simon croaked a laugh. "Those two do-gooders? Frank and I cordially disliked each other. No run-ins, just a different way of seeing the world. One reason we never did business together, and I kept our money at the other bank."

"All right." Rich opened his notebook. "I need to ask you a few questions to help identify the remains."

"Go ahead." The words held a note of caution.

The man sounded reluctant. Why? Shouldn't a bereaved father be eager to identify the remains of his only son?

Nicole guided her car aimlessly through the streets of Ellington, gradually drifting toward the western edge of town. She couldn't stay in the house with her stubbornly silent grandmother one more moment. And a step outside meant viewing yellow crime-scene tape flapping in the breeze. That lovely rose garden had masked a clandestine burial site all these years. Did Grandpa Frank know? How could he? *How could he not?* Maybe the patch of ground had been precious to him because of what lay beneath, not what was planted on top.

On her right, the town graveyard slid past. The baby's remains should have been buried there in dignity. Maybe now the little body would find a proper resting place. But what name would be chiseled on the headstone?

Ahead loomed the fortresslike Elling home. Many folks thought the place grand. Nicole begged to differ. The brick structure resembled a prison more than a home. Even as a child, when her family visited Grandma and Grandpa, and she ran free with the town children, she'd sensed the place wasn't built to welcome folks. It seemed fashioned to hide whatever went on within those thick walls.

The sun dipping toward the horizon picked a glint of red from the top of a black-and-white SUV parked in front of the massive entrance doors at the end of the long driveway. What brought the police chief straight from the bones found at the Keller property to the imposing Elling mansion?

Rich Hendrick's tall, solid frame and bold features appeared in her mind's eye. His green-gold gaze had peered into her soul, seen everything and revealed nothing. Or that's the impression the cop look gave. Nicole knew better, but she'd felt exposed all the same. What if he discerned something that would prove one or both of her grandparents a baby killer? A tiny squeak escaped her tight throat. That was nonsense. Somebody other than Frank or Jan Keller had buried that child. Surely, Rich could see that. Anyone who knew her grandparents would laugh the notion to scorn. Wouldn't they?

While she'd knelt next to him near the grave wrappings, his clean scent and gentle tone had touched an empty, aching place in Nicole's heart. And the silver at the temples of his close-cut sandy hair had begged to be touched. He hadn't been wearing a wedding ring.

She swallowed. Hard. *Idiot!* What was the matter with her?

Nicole turned the car onto a road at right angles to the Elling property and puffed out a long breath. Glen had been gone only six months. Wasn't it too soon to feel attraction for someone else? Besides, she'd vowed never again to get involved with a cop… or any man with a high-risk occupation. Nicole shook herself and squeezed the steering wheel. The shock of her discovery must have made her a little loony.

A thick planting of trees screened the side of the Elling mansion from view. Nicole turned onto a narrow, paved county road that skirted the rear of the large property. The tree line thinned here, and she glimpsed patches of flower-garden colors contrasted against the weathered red brick of the building. A weed-edged approach beckoned between a gap in the trees. Nicole wheeled her small car into the dirt track and stopped, facing the Elling home.

Crossing her arms over the steering wheel, Nicole leaned her chin on one forearm and squinted toward the garden that looked as if it had been left to grow wild. Weed-green poked up amidst the white heads of Shasta daisies and orange tiger lilies. Ivy groped along the face of the building, tendrils drooping over windowpanes like shaggy lashes above dark, brooding eyes. With its location next to the graveyard and unkempt appearance, no wonder the town kids made up stories about this place.

What had she been told one moonlit night when she hung out in a neighboring kid's tree house? They sat in a tight circle, five of them, foreheads nearly touching, warm breath mingling, as ghost stories whispered from lip to lip. "There's a boogeyman in the Ellings' basement," lisped one sharp, eager face. "He steals babies and eats them!"

A remembered shiver passed down Nicole's spine. So deliciously frightening then, so silly now. Or maybe not. Her pulse stalled as images of an infant's remains flashed through her mind. Only the child hadn't been found here. Yet the police chief shot straight to the boogeyman's lair. Was there some nugget of truth in the small-town legend?

Her gaze swept the property. In the midst of the garden, a slumped figure caught her eye, and she stared. A person, yes, but limp and still on a bench.

The head hung low, face covered by what looked like a dark shroud. The figure's shoulders drooped, arms flopped to the sides, as if some life-size rag doll had been flung onto the bench.

Swallowing a sour taste, Nicole eased out of her car and shut the door. The sound drew no movement from the hunched form on the bench. Was the person all right? Did they need help? Nicole's legs carried her without conscious command toward the garden. Breath labored in and out of tight lungs. She prayed she wasn't about to discover another dead body.

Rich held his expression deadpan. "Do you recall what your boy was wearing when he disappeared?"

A blank stare answered him. "Can't say that I do." Simon pursed his lips.

Rich nodded and made a notation. Of course, a guy not remembering what someone was wearing didn't strike him as too surprising.

"How about if any object went missing with him?" Rich held his pen poised.

The man's forehead wound into a knot of wrinkles. "I seem to remember something about an item, but can't recall what it was." He polished off his drink then surged to his feet and stalked toward the wet bar. "Can I get you anything?"

"Sorry. I'm on duty."

Simon snickered. "You wouldn't drink with me anyway."

Rich let silence speak for him.

Simon lifted a decanter and brown liquid glugged into the snifter. "We paid the ransom, and do you know what we got in return?" A muscle twitched in his cheek. "Bubkes!" Simon charged toward the desk, flesh a mottled red. "When a man sinks his whole world into an heir, he ought to get him back, don't you think?"

Rich held himself motionless as Simon ground to a halt inches from his position. The man was almost as tall as Rich, but all bone and sinew, as if his almost eighty years of life had drained the juices from him.

"An heir to carry on the name may not mean much to most people."

Rich's skin tightened. Simon may as well have said *peons* instead of *people*. No wonder this whole family set his teeth on edge.

"But the Ellings *must* have a namesake!" Simon's hiss blew a waft of booze-breath, and Rich took a step back.

The words sounded like a litany Simon rehearsed often in his head, probably passed down from male heir to male heir. Rich made a note on his pad. He hated to break it to the guy, but there weren't any namesakes running around this mausoleum. Nicole

Keller may have unearthed the last of the line in her grandparents' backyard.

Who put the child there—and why—was Rich's business to find out, and Simon's reaction sounded… off. He didn't hear fatherly grief in this man's tone. More like an investor's outrage at a swindle. He'd known Simon was a hard man, but this hard?

Nicole's steps slowed as she neared the hunched figure who sat on a wooden bench beneath the shade of a maple tree. Nicole stopped on the weed-grown remnants of a stone path a few feet away and held her breath. The ample figure indicated that the person was female. She wore a vintage 1950s dress with a wide Peter Pan collar and a full, swing skirt. Nicole wouldn't be surprised if there was a crinoline beneath it. Only one person in town dressed as if they'd never left the era of saddle shoes—Hannah Breyer, Fern Elling's sister. And thank goodness, the woman's chest moved up and down with even breaths. Hannah was asleep, not dead, and the shroud over her face was merely a dark scarf flopped forward in her sleep.

Nicole slowly exhaled. She'd leave Hannah to her nap. Pivoting, Nicole's shoes scraped against the dirt coating the paving stones, and a breath stuttered behind her.

"What?… Oh, my. Who are you?"

Heart sinking, Nicole turned toward Hannah. The

woman brushed her scarf out of her face and back on top of her gray curls. Faded-green eyes squinted up at the intruder.

"I'm sorry to disturb you." Nicole lifted apologetic hands. "It's Nicole Mattson. Er, you probably know me as Keller. I thought…" She hesitated. "You looked…" How did she tell the other woman she'd mistaken her for dead? "Oh, never mind. I was just passing by and stopped to check on you."

"Keller? Really?" A debutante's giggle left Hannah's throat. "How kind of you. Not many folks around here check on this old gal. Have a seat." She patted the bench beside her.

Nicole glanced toward her car, half hidden in the trees, and then back toward Hannah. The poor thing looked so hopeful for human companionship, Nicole didn't have the heart to turn her down, even though her feet wanted to carry her back to her vehicle. She settled on the edge of the bench. A faint lilac scent drifted to her from the other woman.

"Tell me about yourself, Nicole Keller." Hannah's pudgy hand patted Nicole's knee. "My, you've gotten grown up. Are you visiting your grandparents, like usual?"

Nicole stiffened and met Hannah's open gaze. The older woman remembered her? To Nicole's knowledge, they'd only met once, and that was by accident years ago. "I'm staying with Grandma Jan for a while. Grandpa Frank passed away ten years ago."

Hannah's face puckered like a child presented with a puzzle. "Mercy me, how could I forget something like that? Where is my head going to?"

Nicole smiled. "It's all right. He went peacefully in his own bed." Not like her father or her husband. She shook off the pinch of grief.

Sadness drooped Hannah's lips. "He was a good man. A very good man."

"I agree." Nicole clasped her hands together in her lap. Frank Keller had nothing to do with the baby buried under his rose garden. Surely, everyone would know that.

Gentle fingers brushed a sweep of hair from Nicole's cheek. Hannah's green eyes searched her features. "You look troubled, dear. Do you want to talk about it?"

Nicole shrugged, words crowding to her lips. She *did* want to talk, to rant, to pull her hair, maybe even scream. But none of those reactions would change anything. They wouldn't bring her dad back, or her husband, or put that poor child's bones back into the ground where they couldn't cast a shadow over everything that still mattered in her life.

"I was just driving around thinking."

Hannah bobbed her head, scarf tips wagging in rhythm under her full chin. "I do the same thing when I've got something on my mind."

Nicole cast a glance toward the rear door of the house. A small canopy wrapped the portal in deep shadows. What was the police chief in there telling Simon Elling right now? How did the dead child connect with the Ellings? Hannah might know. She was going to find out about Nicole's discovery sooner rather than later.

She dragged her tongue across dry lips. "The contractors dug up something in my grandparents' backyard, and I found it."

Hannah's face lit. "A treasure?"

Nicole shook her head. She tucked her feet under the bench and gripped the seat with both hands.

"You can't leave me in suspense!" The older woman grabbed Nicole's arm. "You simply have to tell me now!"

"I know. But it's…hard." She swallowed. "I found a child's bones." She winced, more from the sound of those terrible words than from the grip that tightened around her arm. "Who would bury a baby in my grandparents' backyard?"

Hannah let out a little squeak and released Nicole. Her eyes, mouth and nostrils all formed round O's. She clasped Nicole in a python's squeeze. "You found him! Baby Sammy's been found at last!"

"Baby Sammy?" Nicole's words came out muffled in Hannah's lilac-scented bosom.

Hannah set her away. Tears streamed into every crevice of the older woman's face. "The dearest little boy on the planet. Little Samuel Elling. He went missing over fifty years ago. I'd given up that he'd be found." Her hands flapped like an excited bird. "We must tell Simon straight away."

She leaped up, but Nicole grabbed her hand. "The police are here already."

"Then we must hurry." Hannah tugged Nicole to her feet. The woman was as strong as she was stout. "I need to see Simon's reaction when he's told his heir has been found. I wouldn't miss that for the world."

"Just a minute. I don't understand."

"You will soon enough." Hannah hurried up the flagstones toward the house. "Come along, dear."

Nicole scurried to keep up. "I don't know if I should. I mean, I'm not family."

"Oh, pish. I'm family and I invited you. You're entitled. After all, you found him."

Joy pulsed from the woman as if Nicole had announced the child was about to be returned alive. Maybe Hannah's muddled mind had misunderstood. But how could she?

When Nicole was a little girl, Grandma Jan had warned her about the people who lived in this house, and the warning had struck deep. Her grandmother wasn't one to speak ill of others. Of course, everyone knew about Melody, the ice queen, and her prima-donna ways. But it wasn't about her that Grandma had cautioned the most. It was Hannah. Grandma gave her orders to stay away from the woman in the funny clothes.

But Nicole hadn't seen a thing to fear in the mixed-up woman—either now or the day she ran into her, literally. Twelve-year-old Nicole had been trotting along on a main street sidewalk eager to meet up with some friends, then boom! She came up short against a stout figure emerging from Darlene's Beauty Shop. The scent of lilac enveloped her then as it had today, and she looked up into the dreaded woman's face, steeled for a scolding. Only Hannah hadn't said one harsh word. She'd asked who Nicole was and seemed pleased to meet the Kellers' grand-daughter. She'd smiled and dug in her purse then swished off up the street, leaving Nicole with a pair of wide eyes and a peppermint in her hand.

Ahead of Nicole, Hannah's crinoline swished exactly the way it had twenty years ago, and the '50s dancing slippers on her feet tapped the stones. She led the way up three steps, pulled open the door and motioned Nicole inside.

Nicole hesitated. She was about to enter the boogeyman's lair. Not that a childhood ghost story had any hold on her now. Her fears had way more substance. What did her grandparents have to do with the missing heir of the town's founding dynasty? Rich might not be happy to see her barging in, but anything she could find out about the investigation might help her discover the truth that would clear her family name.

Or not.

THREE

"I'd like to speak to Fern," Rich said.

"Sorry." Simon tapped his snifter. "My wife is indisposed and has gone to bed."

"You don't think she'd want to be informed of this development as soon as possible?"

Simon took a sip. "Giving birth to our son nearly killed her. After we lost him, she never got over it. Half a century has passed. I won't rob her of sleep over news that can wait until tomorrow. Old scars are going to rip open. *I* want to be the one to break it to her."

Rich studied Simon under lowered brows. Fine-sounding concern for his wife. Only Simon wasn't known for patience with his sickly spouse. The man resumed his seat at the desk and leaned back in his chair, chin lifted. He'd never looked so arrogant... or so closemouthed. Too bad Rich couldn't have videotaped this proceeding for later review. Something stunk around here, but smell wouldn't show up on camera, only in a cop's nose.

"I was hoping she might know something to help with the identification."

Simon shrugged. "Another day."

Rich made a note in his book. "How about Hannah?"

Simon's eyes widened. "What about her?"

"She lived here at the time of the kidnapping, she might remember something useful."

The other man barked a laugh. "Are we talking about the same woman?"

Rich pressed his lips together. Yes, Hannah lived somewhere in the last century, but she wasn't an idiot. "What could it hurt if I asked her?"

The study door burst open, and a plump figure in an old-fashioned dress swept inside, followed by a more hesitant slender woman in jeans. Rich's eyes narrowed. Hannah he might have expected, but what was Nicole doing here? She cast him a side-long glance, and then her gaze moved from Simon to Hannah and back again. Rich followed her look. She was a good observer. The patriarch's face had darkened nearly to the color of his beverage, while Hannah appeared to be walking on air.

Simon rose, chest inflated. "I've warned you about barging into my study uninvited."

The light on Hannah's face dimmed. "I had to come because of the news. Dearest Nicole has found our Sammy."

Rich stifled a sigh. Nicole had spilled the beans.

But why was she here in the first place? His gaze rested on her.

She shifted from one foot to the other. "I was driving around…thinking. And I saw Hannah sitting in the garden. She looked—"

"Like I needed help." Hannah finished for her with a bright chortle. "Wasn't that sweet?" She scurried over to Simon's desk. "Isn't it wonderful about little Sammy?"

Simon scowled. "Wonderful that a baby's bones have been found? We don't know that it's Samuel, and if it is, he's no less lost to us than the day he disappeared."

"But—"

"Contain yourself." Simon's words came out a growl, and Hannah winced then sent a pleading look toward Nicole.

Rich made a mental note. The older woman had formed an instant bond with Nicole. Was it because she found Samuel's remains or because she showed Hannah compassion by stopping to check on her?

Nicole stepped forward, her gaze on Simon. "I know this is terrible news and does nothing to restore your loss, but I don't fault Hannah for being excited about the possibility of closure for your family. Your wife will likely feel the same way." Her gaze slanted toward Rich and then darted away.

Smooth words from the heart of a peacemaker, but she could as well have added aloud, "As long

as that closure doesn't implicate my grandparents."
Rich's gut clenched. Circumstances placed Frank
and Jan at the top of the suspect list. There wasn't
enough hard evidence to make an arrest—yet—but
the community was going to have a field day with
speculations.

Rich poised his pen over his notebook. "As
long as you're here, Hannah, let me ask you a few
questions."

Simon subsided into his chair with a wave that
absolved him of any connection with the discus-
sion he considered a waste of time. Nicole's posture
stiffened.

Rich would just as soon she wasn't privy to any
more information than she needed to be, especially
when the investigation involved her grandparents.
"You should head home, Nicole. I'm sure your grandmother could use the company."

Color rose in her cheeks, and her dark eyes
snapped. "My grandmother has shut herself in her
bedroom and won't talk to me, so I'm not sure what
you think I should be doing for her."

Dismay sent a pang to Rich's heart. "I wasn't criticizing. I meant—"

"I won't say a word without her here." Hannah
wound her arm through Nicole's and clung, jaw
jutting.

Nicole's mouth fell open. It seemed Hannah's

fixation on her was as much a surprise to Nicole as anybody else.

"Very well." Rich nodded. "Hannah, do you remember what Samuel was wearing when he disappeared?"

"When he was cruelly kidnapped from his own bed, don't you mean?" Hannah's gaze turned fierce. "He was in his fuzzy red sleeper with an adorable sheep embroidered on the right shoulder. It was fall, you know, and the air had a nip so we dressed him warmly."

Rich wrote in his book. "And was anything taken with him?"

Hannah cocked her head then nodded. "We never did see his favorite toy again. The kidnappers must have bundled it off with him."

"A toy?" Rich cocked a brow. "Can you describe it?"

"It was a blue-and-white rattle on a stick." Hannah disengaged her arm from Nicole's and made a shaking motion as if she held the toy. "Such a simple plaything made him laugh and coo. The sides were flat, so he liked to bite it while he teethed. Simon and Fern spent loads of money on fancy toys that squeaked or played music or danced or—"

"We get the idea, Hannah." Simon's tone dripped contempt. "Stop rambling and answer the police chief's questions."

Hannah blinked, and her gaze went vague. She

squinted toward Rich. "Chief? You? Aren't you some kind of deputy? What happened to Chief Wilson?"

Rich sent her a gentle smile. "He retired six years ago."

"Oh, that's right." She gave an airy wave. "Time has a way of flying, doesn't it?"

"Thank you, Hannah." Rich shut his notebook. "You've been very helpful."

"Is it Sammy?" The older woman twisted her fingers together.

Nicole touched her arm. "Chief Hendricks won't be able to say yet. They have to run DNA tests."

Rich smiled toward Nicole. The gesture brought no thaw in her wary expression. He couldn't fault her for being defensive about the investigation, but maybe he'd get a chance later to tell her how much he appreciated her discretion in not blurting that the infant's remains had been clothed in red and that a blue-and-white rattle was buried with the body.

"I'd like to get a DNA sample from you, Simon." He nodded toward the older man. "And one from Fern as soon as possible."

Simon rose and set his snifter on the desk. "So basically you're here to question us, collect evidence and offer next to no information in return."

"I'm afraid that's the way it works at this point." And why wasn't Simon falling all over himself to cooperate? Was it simply a power trip? His puzzling behavior nagged at Rich.

Simon crossed his arms over his chest. "I'll have to discuss this testing thing with Fern. We'll get back to you."

Rich's mouth opened then he clamped his teeth together. He wasn't surprised that the frail Mrs. Elling was indisposed, but this was the first time he ever heard of Simon needing to consult his wife about anything.

"I'll do the test," Hannah singsonged. "I'd love to give some DNA. Give generously. Isn't that what they say at the blood drives?"

Simon whirled on his sister-in-law. "DNA testing isn't like giving blood, you ninny."

"Actually, it's simpler." Nicole glared at Simon. "Nothing to be squeamish about."

Rich clicked his pen and swallowed a grin at the spunky woman's implication that the town patriarch had a yellow streak. Simon's eyes popped wide, and his color darkened. Rich opened his mouth to intervene.

"Then let's do it!" Hannah stuck out her tongue at her brother-in-law like an overgrown toddler.

Nicole's gaze met Rich's. Amusement flickered between them, and his insides warmed. Maybe there was still a chance that they could be friends…or something more.

"I'm sorry." Rich looked toward Hannah. "We need DNA from the mother and father for legal certainty of the child's identity."

Hannah's shoulders wilted.

Simon waved her away. "Go polish your nails or something."

Hannah shuffled to the door, Nicole in her wake. On the threshold, Nicole glanced back and their gazes collided. What did he see in her eyes? Pity toward Hannah? Anger toward Simon? Fear of the police investigation? Yes, all of those. Rich was pretty sure if there was any more information to be gleaned from Hannah, Nicole would get it.

But would she share it with him?

Nicole's hands bunched into fists as she trailed Hannah up a dim hallway. The older woman's head hung as if her scarf were a mantle of sorrow. Nicole didn't blame Hannah for chronic depression. If human kindness had ever warmed these rooms, all trace had long since leached away. In Hannah's place, she would have popped Simon one in the snoot—at least in her imagination—and packed her bags. Why *did* the woman stay around? Of course, at her age, the most likely move was an assisted-living facility, and those cost a lot of money that Hannah likely didn't have. The poor woman was trapped.

Nicole moved up alongside her forlorn hostess. "I should be going now. I hadn't intended to stay this long."

"It's all right." Hannah patted Nicole's shoulder. The ghost of a spark lit the older woman's gaze.

Rebellion still lived in the wrinkled old heart, and Nicole silently rejoiced. "Can you show me to the door?"

"I have something I need to give you first." Hannah crooked a finger and entered a small sitting room toward the back of the house "This is my little apartment." She continued through the outer room and into a bedroom done in pale pink chintz. More like a child's room than an adult's with the frilly canopy over a twin bed and a ballerina theme.

Hannah stood on tiptoe and twirled, full skirt billowing. "You can see what I once dreamed of doing."

Nicole nodded, mute. She understood squashed dreams. She and Glen had wanted children in the worst way, but—Nicole stuffed the pain back into its hidey-hole. Too raw to deal with at this inconvenient moment. But when would the convenient time come?

"This way." Hannah waved her over to a gaily painted trunk at the foot of the bed. She rummaged inside and came out with a blue satin drawstring bag. "Here." She held it out.

"Oh, I couldn't—"

Hannah placed a pudgy finger over Nicole's lips. "This was Sammy's. My keepsake of him. Give it to Chief Wilson."

Nicole swallowed the urge to correct her on the

chief's identity. What was the point? She peeped inside the bag. It contained an infant's hair brush.

Her heart rate sprang into a jog-trot. "I'll pass this along."

"Good." Hannah winked. "The back door is up the hall and to the left." The woman stretched and yawned. "I'm very tired now. I think I'll turn in."

Nicole carried her small treasure toward the exit. Hannah must be sharper than anyone gave her credit for if she realized the hairs in the brush might positively identify her precious nephew, with or without parental DNA.

Nicole passed through a pristine, stainless-steel kitchen and shivered. Clean, cold and efficient. Like the people who lived here. Except she got the feeling that beneath the polish of prestige the filth ran deep. Sort of like the Pharisees Jesus called "white-washed tombs." Maybe she'd found baby Samuel Elling's remains beneath her grandparents' rose garden, but what if the truth behind the death was buried within these brick walls?

Simon inhaled his last gulp of brandy. "Why don't you come back another time, and we'll see about that DNA." The man's eyes flashed a message that the interview was over.

Rich's fingers itched to snatch the glass out of Simon's hand. That item would do very nicely for DNA, but he had no choice except to leave. For now.

He jerked his chin toward the Elling patriarch. "I'll stay in touch."

"Be sure you do. Maybe I'll give Judge Becker a call. Let him know you're on top of a hot case and need your docket cleared."

"That won't be necessary. I'll visit with the D.A. in the morning." If Simon Elling could play the old-buddy card with his lifelong pal, Judge Becker, Rich could remind him that the prosecuting attorney was from a different era and not in his pocket. And it was the D.A. he'd report developments to, not to either of the judges that served the county, especially not Becker.

Rich saw himself to the door, footsteps echoing in the empty foyer. He'd known this family was strange, but why would Simon balk at the surest way to prove his son had been found? He needed to look at the case file from the time of the kidnapping and see how closely family had been looked at as suspects. The personal touches in the clandestine burial indicated some level of caring. Of course, he hadn't seen any such thing in the hard eyes of Simon Elling.

Dusk had gripped the land when Rich stepped outside. He deeply inhaled the cooling air, relieved to be out of that house's oppressive atmosphere. He went down the stairs and up the walk toward his vehicle. At the curb, Rich did a one-eighty observation of the property. As he turned toward the house, a curtain moved in a lit room upstairs. Fern or Melody?

The roar of a motor drew his attention. Headlights barreled up the driveway toward him, and a low-slung sports car rumbled to a halt behind his SUV. A male figure climbed out of the passenger side. Mason Wright. *Now the gang's all here.* Rich hooked a thumb in his front jeans pocket and watched the young man move toward him, swaying as if he were a sailor at sea. Three sheets to the wind all right, and it wasn't even 10:00 p.m.

If Mason had been behind the wheel, Rich could have arrested him. Maybe this third time would have been the charm, and the D.U.I. would stick. Or maybe not, if Judge Becker heard the case. The Elling fortunes might be in the tank, but their influence still loomed large.

Whip-slender and inches shorter than Rich's six feet one, Melody's son halted in front of Rich and snapped a sloppy salute. "If it ain't the chief. Come to harash me again? Shorry to dishappoint you." The twenty-six-year-old delinquent burped in Rich's face.

"I think you've disappointed yourself enough for the both of us." Rich went to the sports car and knocked on the window.

The glass whooshed down, and Taylor Mead, Dr. Sharla's daughter and Mason's newest girlfriend, stared up at him. "Don't mind me, Chief, I'm clean and sober." Her gaze fell away.

Rich shook his head. She'd probably had a soft drink, that was the kind of girl she was. But how long would she maintain her standards if she hung around Mason and his crowd? The doctor's family went to the same little community church that Rich did. He'd taught Taylor in youth group, and she was a classmate of his daughter Katrina's, though not a close friend.

He leaned closer. "Does your mom know you're rocketing around in this death trap with a drunken passenger?"

Taylor glared. "Hey, he called me up and asked me to drive him home from Sparky's Bar. He knows you guys are waiting for him to slip up again. He's not so bad, you know. Just needs someone to understand him."

Right. He'd heard that same song from women with black eyes and busted jaws, courtesy of the poor, misunderstood dirtball they called boy-friend or husband. He didn't want Taylor to end up another statistic. Mason was known to have the Elling temper.

"At least let me give you a lift back to your own car." Rich offered a smile.

She tucked her lower lip between straight white teeth that must have cost her folks a hunk of change, and then shook her head. Her gaze was fixed on the young man who stood swaying on the entrance walk.

"I'll probably hang out here awhile. Play video games. Whatever." She opened the car door, and Rich stepped out of the way as she emerged. "I'm nineteen years old and headed for college in a few weeks. I appreciate your concern, but you and my parents will have to stop mother-henning me." She flipped her blond hair over her shoulder and stomped off.

"If you think you need a ride," he spoke after her, "call me no matter what time it is."

Heart heavy, he got into his SUV. Something was seriously funky in that household, and a bright girl with a promising future like Taylor didn't belong in all that darkness. But he couldn't control her choices. Just like he couldn't control Jan Keller's choice not to tell him what she knew about the baby that was buried in her backyard.

He guided his vehicle out of the driveway and onto one of the torn-up city streets. Behind him a pair of headlights came up quickly, bouncing over the bumpy track. Whoever it was needed to slow down and keep their distance. Frowning, Rich's hand moved toward the control for his bubble lights, then froze. The car behind flashed its headlights and signaled to pull over. Rich eased to the side of the road, and the other vehicle stopped behind him. The car's door opened, and the dome light revealed Nicole climbing out. Rich met her between their vehicles. The headlights from her car outlined her figure but left her features in shadows.

"Hi." He ventured a small wave. "Thanks for handling matters so well back there."

She let out a small laugh. "Here, I thought you were going to scold me for horning in on the investigation."

"I probably should, but I get the sense that you were caught up in the moment and ended up where you didn't expect."

Her shoulders slumped. "The whole day has been like that. More like the past year."

Was something heavy going on in Nicole's life even before her husband was killed? Rich stopped the question from popping out of his mouth. He didn't have the right to ask anything like that yet.

"What have you got there?" He motioned toward a bag she cupped in a palm as if it were fragile and precious.

"I was waiting at the intersection up the street for you to leave the Ellings so I could give you this. It's from Hannah. Baby Samuel's hairbrush. Maybe there's still usable DNA on it." Nicole held the bag out to him.

Rich let out a low whistle and took the offering. "Thanks. I knew you'd handle Hannah like a pro."

"No handling necessary." She crossed her arms.

"She volunteered. At least one person in that house wants the poor child identified."

Rich nodded. "We need an ID to have any hope of finding out who might have buried the infant on your grandparents' property."

"You're giving them the benefit of the doubt?"

Her breathless hope sent a shaft through Rich's heart. He steeled his emotions. "No more than I would any other citizen in good standing. Innocent until proven guilty, remember?"

She cleared her throat. "Well, thanks for that anyway."

An awkward silence stretched between them.

"Good night," she ventured first and turned away.

"Good night," Rich called after her.

Good night? He climbed into his SUV. What a joke!

Nicole's discovery could steamroll her whole family under the wheels of justice. Unfortunately, he was the guy that had to drive the steamroller whichever direction the investigation led. Neither of them was going to sleep well tonight.

Nicole tossed and turned in her upstairs bedroom. The last time she looked at the bedside clock, it was nearing midnight. There was no way that Grandpa Jan or Grandpa Frank had anything to do with her horrific discovery. They were so honest they'd go out of their way to return a dime if a checkout clerk gave them too much change. But then why was an infant buried beneath Grandpa Frank's roses?

And what was the matter with her that she'd taken note of that police chief's naked wedding ring finger? What a time to suddenly feel attraction for a man. The shock of her discovery must have affected her even worse than she thought if a square chin and a pair of vivid hazel eyes could jump-start her pulse.

Had he always been single? Or was he divorced like too many cops? Maybe widowed? That would be a switch, the spouse going before the cop, but it happened. His voice had been strong, yet gentle when examining the remains. He'd been firm when questioning her grandmother, though, but not bullying, like some behaved with suspects.

Suspects! Her grandmother was a suspect in the death of a baby. Unbelievable! Her grandfather, too. He might be dead and gone, but this discovery promised to assassinate the memory of his character. Unless he was clearly exonerated. Unless they both were.

Nicole caught her breath. *Please, God, let this mystery be solved.* But what if the case remained unsolved and suspicion clouded the rest of her grandmother's days? *And let my grandparents be innocent.* But what if they weren't?

Sighing, Nicole sat up and switched on the small table lamp. She might as well go downstairs and warm a cup of milk. The old-fashioned remedy had helped many nights when Glen was out on night duty, and she knew he had a particularly dangerous case on his docket.

Nicole threw on her robe and padded barefoot down the carpeted stairs, relying on the nightlights her grandmother had strategically placed along the route for vision. She stepped off the hallway carpet onto the cool kitchen linoleum, and the sound of stealthy footfalls on the porch froze her in her tracks. She'd read in the local newspaper about a rash of nighttime thefts in the county. Her heart did a somersault.

Had they forgotten to lock the door?

The door latch clicked, and the panel creaked slowly ajar.

FOUR

"Grandma!" Nicole blurted the word on a gust of pent-up breath.

The nightlight over the sink outlined the full figure who stepped inside. Grandma Jan let out a squeak and pressed a hand to her chest.

Nicole stepped farther into the kitchen. "What in the world are you doing outside in the middle of the night?" Had she been poking around in the crime scene? But no dirt showed on the woman's robe, nightgown or slippers.

"Aw, honey, you nearly scared me out of my skin."

Nicole gurgled a laugh. "You did the same for me, sneaking around like that."

Grandma Jan's posture stiffened. "I wasn't sneaking. Couldn't sleep so I went outside for some fresh air. What are you doing up this time of night?"

"I couldn't sleep, either, so I thought maybe a glass of warm milk would help." Nicole went to the refrigerator. "Would you like one?"

Her grandmother patted her on the shoulder. "No, thanks, dear. I think I'll try to catch forty winks now."

Nicole turned and watched her pad away. Was that a note of relief she'd caught on the other woman's voice? Like she'd successfully accomplished a secret mission? Nicole shrugged. She was always second-guessing people's reactions and motives. Hazard of being a cop's daughter and a cop's wife. She needed to get out of that habit. She wasn't going to get caught up in that way of life anymore. Another reason to kick herself for checking out that fine-looking police chief. Available or not, he was off-limits as far as her wounded heart was concerned.

She thunked a mug onto the counter more briskly than she'd intended and winced at the noise. Then the milk came out of the jug faster than she'd antici-pated and slopped over the edge of the cup. Nicole made an exasperated sound, wiped the counter with a paper towel and threw it in the wastebasket under the sink.

That's funny. An empty trash bag lined the con-tainer. Last night before she went to bed, she'd made a mental note that the full garbage bag needed to be taken out to the large trash bin in the alley bright and early in the morning before the city truck came by to pick it up. Her grandmother must have taken the trash out as part of her midnight wanderings.

On one hand, finding something productive to do

if she wasn't able to sleep would be just like Grandma Jan. On the other, what had her grandmother been looking for in her bedroom right after the gruesome discovery? Some sort of evidence that had to do with the bones that were found? Did she dispose of the article in the trash? If so, why wait until the middle of the night? Grandma could have taken out the trash while Nicole was gadding around town in her car. But maybe Grandma couldn't decide what to do with whatever it was she wanted to hide? Maybe it had taken her until the middle of the night to make up her mind to destroy it?

Nerves quivered beneath Nicole's skin. Digging through a garbage bag in the wee hours was not an appealing prospect, but she needed to assure herself that her suspicions were baseless. But what if they weren't? Then she needed to get at the truth. A baby was dead. Someone had to be held accountable. Her ingrained sense of justice wouldn't allow any alternative.

Abandoning her milk on the counter, Nicole grabbed a flashlight from on top of the refrigerator and went to the back door. She glanced down at her bare feet. No help for that now. She wasn't going back upstairs for her slippers. And even the flashlight was pushing it for a light source since Grandma's room faced toward the garage and alley. Nicole didn't want her grandmother to suspect she was checking up on her.

The outside air was still muggy after the warm summer day, but a breeze ruffled Nicole's pajama pants as she soft-footed down the deck stairs. Grit on the sidewalk stuck to the bottoms of her feet as she hustled toward the alley. A three-quarter moon lit her way, so she didn't bother with the flashlight. The single-car garage that housed her grandmother's late-model Chevy loomed to her right, and beyond the building at the end of the short driveway squatted the large, plastic trash bin.

Nicole stopped at the bin and glanced around. The house across the alley lay in darkness. To her right, she made out the arced form of her compact car sitting on a cement pad. To her left, the wind rustled the leaves on a hedge of bushes that lined the Keller property on the alley side. The neighborhood lay quiet. Not even a dog barked at this time of night.

She eased open the lid of the garbage can, and a rush of foul smell attacked her nostrils from years of trash passing through its confines. Using the lid as a shield, she pointed her flashlight down into the container. Her eyes widened. The can was empty. Nicole's gaze quickly scanned the area again. Nothing out of place. Certainly nothing that resembled a stray trash bag. What had her grandmother done with the garbage from the kitchen?

Nicole shifted her stance, and a pebble nipped her heel. She let out a grunt of pain. Why was she standing out here in the pitch dark in her pajamas and bare feet, hunting for a sack of refuse? Because she couldn't stand a mystery unsolved, that was why. The only other place she could think to look was the garage. A few steps took her to the side garage door. She twisted the knob, but it didn't budge.

Grandma told her she'd started locking the garage at night since the rash of petty thefts had resulted in people losing lawn mowers, leaf blowers, snow-mobiles and even motorcycles.

Nicole blew out a breath that ruffled her bangs. So much for plan A. She'd just have to move on to plan B. Squaring her shoulders, she headed back to the house.

A few hours later, her fitful slumber was blasted by the shrill of her alarm clock. Moaning, Nicole groped for the shut-off switch…or maybe she should just press the snooze button. She forced herself to sit up straight. Dawn light filtered around the blinds on the bedroom window. As much as she could use a little more shut-eye, she needed to hunt for that garbage bag while her grandmother was still in bed.

Nicole threw on a blouse, denim capris, ankle socks and tennis shoes. Halfway down the stairs, she halted and groaned. Plan B was shot, too. A distinctive smell wafted from the kitchen. Bacon. And her grandmother's tuneless hum accompanied the sound of frying. Nicole continued down the stairs.

Grandma's humming ceased. "Pancakes or waffles?" her voice called before Nicole showed her face in the kitchen.

Shaking her head, Nicole leaned her shoulder against the doorjamb. "Worms."

Her grandmother turned from the stove, brows lifted.

Nicole chuckled. "Isn't that what the early bird is always after?"

Grandma laughed and turned a slice of bacon in the frying pan.

"Waffles, please. You know I love those." Nicole headed for the brew in the carafe beside the automatic drip coffee-maker. One of the few gadgets of which her grandmother approved—other than the electric sewing machine.

"Waffles it is, then."

Forty-five minutes later, they cleared the meal dishes from the table, and Nicole still hadn't had a chance to go outside. Conversation had been sporadic small talk. The garbage truck was due any minute.

"I'd better take the trash out," she said as she ran wash water in the sink. No dishwasher in Jan Keller's house, of course. She held her breath for her grandmother's response.

"Already done, dear," the woman answered, face serene.

Nicole ducked her head and squirted dishwashing liquid into the warm water. She hadn't realized her grandmother was such a stellar actress. What did that say about her claims to know nothing about the bones in the garden?

Outside, the rumble of a truck announced that the garbage truck had reached their alley. Sounds of garbage collection continued as Nicole washed the dishes and her grandmother dried.

"Slow down, dear," Grandma said. "I know you want to get over to the shop, but it's early yet."

Truck noises retreated down the alleyway. Nicole's grandmother hung her dish towel on a bar over the sink and squirted lotion onto her hands from the bottle on the counter. A wide smile stretched her lips. "I think I'll go back to bed for a while and join you at the shop later." The woman stretched and left the room with a sprightly tread.

Nicole gazed after her, frowning. Grandma was way too happy about something. Did she think the garbage bag had been taken by the city truck? If so, where was the bag when Nicole looked for it last night? Had someone removed it from the trash bin after Grandma Jan put it in there and before Nicole went outside? A tiny shiver shook her.

Whoever had disposed of that infant's remains could still be in the community. Were they watching the house? That person might do anything to keep from being exposed.

A few ticks before 8:00 a.m., Rich pulled his SUV into the alley outside the Keller home with

Derek Hanson—a young, rookie cop, but a sharp one—in the passenger seat. Behind him, Terry's black-and-white cruised to a halt. The little Ford on the parking pad by the garage was just backing up. The car halted, and Nicole got out, staring at the police vehicles.

Rich stepped toward her and pulled a pair of documents from the pocket of his uniform shirt. "We've got warrants to search the Keller home and the shop."

A tentative smile morphed into a scowl. Nicole waved toward the house. "Grandma's barely stirring, and I was just headed for the shop. What in the world do you expect to find?" Dressed in tan slacks and a print blouse, she came around her car and stopped in front of Rich. Her lips were pressed into a tight line as if restraining herself from saying more.

He gazed into her shuttered face. "The remains were found on Keller property. The judge agreed it would be due diligence to conduct a thorough search of the premises."

"But why the shop, too?" She put her hands on her slender waist.

The other officers flanked him. Terry stuck his thumbs in his belt and rocked back on the heels of his cowboy boots. "Mornin', Nicole. We got a job to do. *I'm* glad we caught you home."

The inflection on *I'm* suggested a personal interest

without strictly flirting. Rich shot the man a sharp look. Then he turned toward Nicole.

"The fabric from Jan's store plays into the case. I know it's a long shot, but that baby deserves every chance for justice."

Her gaze softened. "I agree. My heart bleeds for that child...for the parents. We need to find out who did this, but I don't want—" She halted and licked her lips, a wordless dread flickering in her deep brown eyes.

Rich's gut clenched. She had to have picked up on the fact that her grandmother was hiding something. That put her in a bad predicament—torn between compassion for the dead infant and fear for the fate of her living grandmother.

The deputies moved off toward the back door. Nicole's expression firmed. Scowling, she darted in front of them.

"Hold it!" She put up a forestalling hand. "I won't have you barging in on Grandma Jan. I'll go get her."

"We'll accompany you," Rich said evenly. "But, yes, you can let her know we're here."

"You might have told me last night that you were planning this," she shot back.

Terry sent him a startled look that Rich chose to ignore.

Nicole marched up the sidewalk ahead of them. Striding beside him, Terry's gaze was glued to her swaying hips. Rich jostled his shoulder, and the man answered with a slick grin. Rich frowned him down. What the guy did off duty was one thing, but they were on the clock. Never mind that he didn't like anyone eyeing a class act like Nicole with such sleazy eyes.

They went into the Keller house. The kitchen was neat and clean, and smelled like bacon. Rich's stomach muttered a complaint. He hadn't felt like eating much breakfast this morning. He'd known this search was going to give him a major black eye with Nicole.

"Grandma," she called as they neared a doorway. "We have visitors." The way she spat the last word, she might as well have said *intruders*.

"Oh, really? Who, dear?" The older woman stepped out of her room, dressed in casual pants and a button-up shirt, and pulling a brush through her thinning white hair. Her eyes grew big, and then she smiled. "I suppose you're here to search. We'll get out of your way."

Rich narrowed his eyes. Janet Keller was as chipper today as she'd been obstructive yesterday. Had he already missed the boat on discovering evidence? If so, then Jan not only knew something about the dead child, she had deliberately destroyed evidence. Rich's jaw clenched. He hadn't been able to get in touch with Judge Christy for the warrant before this morning. Yes, he might have tried Judge Becker last night, but he'd just as soon leave Simon Elling's crony as far out of this case as he could.

Nicole and her grandmother went outside, and he and his deputies got to work. A couple of fruitless hours later, he stepped out to find the women seated at the small porch table sharing coffee and donuts from a convenience store down the street.

Nicole avoided his gaze, but Jan beamed at him. "What did you find?" She nodded toward the yellowed newspaper clippings he held in his hand.

"Nothing I plan to take along. I've got copies of these and more in my file back at the office. I thought Nicole might find them of interest."

Nicole accepted the sheaf of clippings. "What are they?"

"You can draw your own conclusions. We found them in a trunk in the attic."

Unfortunately, there was nothing incriminating about an older resident of the area hanging on to news clippings about the kidnapping. It was the most sensational event to happen in the area since the railroad came through. Reading those ought to enlighten Nicole.

Terry and Derek clomped down the porch steps. Terry threw one of his lady-killer smiles toward Nicole. If she saw the look, she didn't respond. Good for her.

"We're heading for the shop now," Rich said.

"Wait!" Nicole lunged from her seat. "I'll go with you to unlock the door."

"I was going to ask for a key, not use a crowbar."

She sniffed and turned toward her grandmother. "Just hang tight until I get back. We'll straighten the mess together."

"Mess?" Jan blinked.

"Cleaning up after themselves is not in search protocol."

The woman responded with a faint "oh," and Nicole headed for her car.

Rich followed her down the steps and caught up with his deputies.

"Feisty, ain't she," Terry said out of the corner of his mouth. "That's the best kind."

"Don't push my buttons today, Bender."

"Okay, Chief. But I was just sayin'…" With an elaborate shrug, he got into his car.

Rich followed Nicole's little Ford into the alley behind the shop that was located on the corner of Ellington's brief main street. He stopped his vehicle beside hers. Without a word, she unlocked the back door and stepped aside while he and his deputies went in. She'd admitted him into a combination storeroom and workroom. A sewing machine, a dressmaker's dummy, and a table laden with bolts of fabric, scissors, measuring tape and other utensils sat on one side of the area. The other end of the long room was occupied by stacks of boxes.

Nicole poked her head inside. "I guarantee you won't find anything. I've been cleaning and sorting and throwing since I got here—practically over my grandmother's dead body." She stopped on a little gasp. "Poor choice of words." She paused. "Anyway, the boxes contain old financial records. I doubt my grandmother ever threw away a slip of paper. If those trip your trigger, go for it." She closed the door just shy of a slam.

Chest tightening, Rich turned toward the stacked banker's boxes. If the ransom from the kidnapping was laundered through the shop, he could be staring at the evidence.

An hour later, they finished going through the store without finding anything else of interest. He loaded his deputies down with boxes of the shop's financial records. Amazing that anyone kept records so far back, but his search of the Keller house had proven that Jan was a pack rat of the first order. That attic must still contain every toy that her son, Henry, Nicole's father, ever played with. There was an impressive box of baseball cards, too. When this case was over, he might clue Nicole in that her grandmother could be sitting on a gold mine in those, as well as the antique toys.

They stepped out the door, and Rich spotted Nicole perched on the hood of her car in the shade of the building. She was reading the yellowed news articles.

"You stuck around?" he said.

She hopped up. "The shop isn't big. I figured it wouldn't take you long, and then I could inspect the damage."

"I'm sorry we have to pull things apart like that, but—"

"I know. It's your job." She waved the sheaf of clippings. "This is a tragic story."

"Very." He didn't add that the Ellings' legacy of sorrow seemed to be passed from one generation to the next—mostly self-inflicted.

"Looks like you decided those old records are of interest." She nodded toward the two boxes he carried and the ones his deputies were loading in the back of the SUV.

"Just taking another long shot." He smiled at her.

She smiled back. Not very big and a bit ruefully, but the minor thaw sent his pulse trip-hammering. What might a full-blown grin from her do to his insides? As he stowed his boxes in the SUV, he prayed that he never had to arrest Jan Keller and rob himself forever of the chance to find out.

Nicole spent a few minutes inspecting the inside of the shop. Most of the mess consisted of things pulled out of place, and the stock would need to be reshelved. She could set things to rights today, and they could probably open up again tomorrow. First, she needed to head home and check on Grandma. She didn't trust that woman not to be doing more than she should to restore order to the house. Nicole locked the back door of the shop and climbed into her car.

On the drive home, a pair of compassionate hazel eyes haunted her. It had really bothered Rich to intrude on their lives, but he'd performed his job thoroughly and professionally. He was the kind of cop who took his oath to protect and to serve seriously. The young cop hadn't said a word, but his demeanor had been respectful toward her and his boss. That over-the-hill peacock, Terry Bender, was another story. He was the dime-a-dozen kind that enjoyed issuing tickets, harassing people and wowing the ladies with his authority. And for some reason, he resented Rich. Did he think *he* should be the chief? Heaven help Ellington if that ever happened!

A few minutes later, Nicole stepped into a silent house. "Grandma, where are you?" Her call went unanswered.

Did her grandmother go to the store for something? Nicole walked into the living room. Papers were strewn everywhere, and furniture was out of place. Thankfully, her grandmother hadn't attempted to put things back by herself. She called out again.

A faint noise overhead brought an exasperated puff of breath.

Grandma had started in the attic. Not the order she would have done things, but her grandmother had always been protective of that eclectic collection of junk up there. What a relief that Rich and his deputies hadn't found anything incriminating in their search of her memorabilia. If there'd been anything to find, Nicole would have guessed it to be up there or in her grandmother's room—that is, if she hadn't already disposed of whatever it was.

Nicole climbed to the second floor then headed up the hall toward the open attic door. Another scrape from above quickened her steps. "Grandma, you stop trying to move things around by yourself. I'm coming."

She was going to have a heart-to-heart with that woman. This was not a situation for her grandmother to try to hide anything she knew—regardless of who she might be protecting. Even if it was herself.

The scent of hot dust greeted Nicole as she climbed high enough to poke her head above the hardwood floor. The mess up here didn't look all that much different than before the search. Towers of boxes and jumbles of toys and discarded household items lay everywhere. Dust motes danced in the humid air in front of the nearest dormer window.

"Grandma?"

She reached the top of the stairs. A movement

caught the corner of her eye, and she started to turn, but a heavy weight of fabric descended over her, choking sound and cutting off sight. A shove sent her into the nearest cluster of junk. She tripped, her scream muffled, and hit the floor hard. Unseen objects poked viciously into her chest and side. Things tumbled around her, striking her back and legs.

Heart hammering against her ribs, Nicole fought the suffocating blanket as footsteps thudded down the stairs. At last her flailing arms succeeded in throwing off the covering. It was an old, ragged quilt that used to grace her grandmother's bed when Nicole would visit as a child. Nicole sat up sharply. Where *was* her grandmother?

Ignoring aches and abrasions, Nicole grasped the edge of an open trunk and hauled herself to her feet. She stared around, panting, but didn't see anyone. Had the burglar done something with Grandma Jan? Or maybe Grandma walked somewhere and wasn't home when someone entered.

Please, God, let that be so.

Nicole needed to get to a phone right away and call for help. She turned toward the stairs, but a tumbled stack of junk blocked her path. She'd have to find a different way to the exit. An opening to her left beckoned, and she followed it. Her feet struck a soft object, and she halted.

She looked down, and a scream rent her

throat. Nicole's grandmother sprawled facedown and motionless. A pool of deep crimson haloed her white head.

FIVE

The ambulance call blared through Rich's car radio. He turned on the siren, cramped the wheel, and did a U-turn at the end of Ellington's main street. Lunch with the downtown crowd hit the bottom of the priority list. He could schmooze and gauge community reaction to the discovery of a baby's remains later.

Someone unconscious and unresponsive at the Keller home? Who? Jan...or Nicole? Bile burned its way up Rich's windpipe.

He slammed to a stop near the telltale trench and leaped from his vehicle while the SUV swayed on its springs. Once again, he was first on the scene, though an ambulance siren had begun to wail in the distance. The back doorknob responded to his touch, and he stepped into the kitchen calling Nicole's name.

"Up here" came a faint response.

Warm relief loosened Rich's muscles. Nicole wasn't injured then. Jan must be the victim. Had the recent excitement given her a heart attack? Maybe guilt had done that.

Rich took the stairs two at a time. Moments later, he poked his head into the attic and saw no one, just tornado-strewn mess. Boy, they really had done a job on this place.

"Nicole?"

"Behind the boxes." Her tone leaked tears.

Picking his way through the junk, Rich rounded a corner. Nicole knelt by the prone form of her grand-mother, pressing a red-stained towel to the woman's head.

Rich stepped closer. "Did she fall?"

"Pushed maybe. Or struck with something. I don't know." Nicole's gaze never left her grandmother. "We had an intruder. He shoved me down, too."

Electricity jolted through Rich. Someone had attacked both women? "Did you get a look at him?"

Nicole shook her head. "He threw a quilt over my head from behind before he tossed me into a pile of junk. Grandma might have seen him, but she's—" A sob left her throat. "She doesn't look good."

Nicole was right. Jan Keller's face had lost all color, and her breathing was shallow at best. The ambulance siren wailed up the street outside.

"Help is here," he said. "You're doing the right thing for the bleeding. Let me look around quick for some sort of weapon before the EMTs crowd in."

Nicole lifted her head and met his gaze. Her reddened eyes brimmed with trust and gratitude. "You'll catch whoever did this."

Rich's insides melted. He'd go after any monster to see that look on her face again. Clearing his throat, he let his gaze roam the stuffy cave beneath the rafters. Yesterday's search and today's scuffle rendered hope of finding clear footprints on the dusty floor useless.

He stepped this way and that, peering over and around objects. This incident could be a common burglary, but what kind of burglar strikes in the daytime? Had a baby killer been stirred to action? Anyone who would kidnap and kill an infant wouldn't balk at a senior citizen. Did the perp come here to silence Jan Keller? Or were they looking for something and Jan interrupted them? Did they find what they wanted? Had Rich's search team overlooked something significant this morning? Questions pummeled him.

Voices came from below. Rich called to the emergency crew and feet sounded on the stairs. He turned another corner. A baseball bat lay on top of a pile of books, like someone had tossed it there. Wet red smears on the end that would normally connect with a ball suggested that it had recently connected with something—or someone—else.

Calm EMTs' voices mingled with Nicole's agitated tones. Equipment snapped and rattled as medical jargon batted back and forth. A soft sob from Nicole called his feet to return to her and offer a pair of strong arms. Duty sent his hand to his belt radio.

"Terry, you got a copy? Where are you?"

"Here with Nicole. Where are you?"

The deputy's voice came through the radio and into Rich's ears from a few feet away. *He* was with Nicole? Leave it to Terry to hover near a beautiful woman. But at least the guy was on top of the case. He'd probably heard the location of the ambulance call and come a' running on instinct just like his chief. Good cop work. Then why did Rich feel so irritated?

He tucked his radio back into it's belt pouch. "Follow my voice, Terry. I've got something you need to see."

Seconds later, Terry appeared and halted on a low curse. "Somebody played baseball with an old lady's head."

A feminine whimper turned both their heads. Nicole stood behind them, staring at the bat. "How could anyone—" Hand clamped over her mouth, she turned and hurried away.

Nausea rolled Rich's gut. Too bad Nicole's curiosity drove her to see that ugly object. Conversation from the EMTs indicated they were getting ready to move their patient. Nicole would no doubt accompany them.

"This connected with the baby discovery, you think?" Terry claimed Rich's attention.

"Could be a common break-in. Maybe the thief thought no one was home after we drove away this morning."

Terry snorted. "And maybe I'm a monkey's uncle."

"Just keeping an open mind. That MBCA tech should hit town any minute. The office'll send him straight here. Let him collect the evidence." He nodded toward the bat. "I'm going to call everyone in—on duty, off duty, on the moon—I don't care. When they get here, organize a canvas of the neighborhood to see if anyone saw someone other than the residents or us enter or leave this house."

Terry's shoulders squared. "Will do, Chief. Where are you going to be?"

"At the hospital, waiting to see how things go with Jan Keller. Maybe she'll wake up and tell us something."

"You might get to do some hand-holding with the granddaughter while you're at it."

Rich didn't dignify the remark with an answer as he walked away.

Nicole paced the hospital waiting room, her stomach in knots. Under lowered brows, she eyed the hallway. No sign of medical staff. They must still be in with her grandmother. What was taking so long?

She checked her watch and let out a long breath. Only three minutes had passed since they wheeled the inert form of her grandmother into the CAT scan room. The passage of time felt like an aeon.

A solid figure blocked her view, extending a paper cup. Rich, bearing a glass of water. He'd trailed the ambulance to the hospital. Nicole took the cup and sipped. Cool moisture soothed her parched throat.

"Thank you." Her words came out a husky whisper.

"Welcome." His sober, intent gaze studied her. "Let me know when you're ready to talk about what happened. Maybe you noticed something helpful and don't realize it yet."

"Sure." Nicole stared into her water. The liquid quivered with the tremor of her hand.

Why was this cop being so nice to her? He must be about ready to bust wide open with the usual barrage of investigator questions. Did he think he could soften her up to betray her grandmother with some revelation, if he let her stew long enough? Or maybe he knew she was too savvy about cops' ways to fall for the usual methods. While she couldn't be a suspect in the baby's death, he probably figured she was privy to her grandmother's secrets. Whether Rich believed it or not, she was just as frustrated as he must be to figure out what her grandmother was hiding.

There was no way Nicole could think Grandma

Jan would hurt a baby. Or Grandpa Frank, either. Not the woman who baked sugar cookies for her or the man who soothed her ouchies when she came to visit. But then, hadn't her father and her husband run into case after case of the most ordinary-seeming people—normally gentle folks—who turned out to have committed the most horrible crimes?

Nicole sank onto a chair and downed the rest of the water. If Rich was letting her soften up by stewing in her own juices, he was doing a great job of it. His gentle gaze remained fixed on her. She looked away. If she lost Grandma Jan to death…or prison, she'd have no one.

Except God.

Her spine stiffened. Sure, she still uttered prayers from time to time out of lifelong habit, but she'd been struggling with her faith for years, ever since her dad died. She knew God existed. She knew He loved people—in theory. She just didn't feel close to Him anymore, not like she had when she was a child.

Nicole licked a trace of moisture from her upper lip. Salty. Not from the cup she held. Tears had fallen without her knowledge. A warm presence settled in the chair next to her. Nicole held herself stiff.

"I want her to be innocent," Rich said. "But I think you know and I know that she's concealing something that might have put her, and possibly you, in danger."

Nicole lifted her gaze to meet his. Today he wore his uniform—gun, badge and all—and looked mighty fine in it.

"Do you think she's protecting someone?" Nicole asked. The most obvious answer was Grandpa Frank, or at least his memory. But in light of the attack, that conclusion didn't totally add up. "If Grandma's trying to hide her own guilt, or Grandpa's, then who came after her today, and why would she protect such a person?"

"Assuming the assault is related to the baby's remains, that's an excellent question. We need to find the answer in order to be assured of her safety… and yours."

Warmth seeped into Nicole's fear-chilled bones. He said "we," as if he included her as a valued participant in the investigation. Maybe that was simply another clever ploy to soften her up some more, but she didn't get the sense that Rich was playing a cop game with her. His hazel gaze was steady and sincere. If her meager tidbits of observation would help catch whoever hurt her grandmother, she had to let this man have them. She could start with a few things directly related to the attack.

"From the way the quilt landed on me and the heaviness of the footfalls on the attic stairs as they ran away, the intruder must have been either a tallish, athletic woman or a slight man."

"Good observation." Rich plucked a notebook from his shirt pocket and scribbled.

Now she had to decide whether to tell him the rest of what she could. Exhaling a deep sigh, she arced the crumpled paper cup into the wastebasket a few feet away.

"Two points." A small smile spread Rich's lips.

She could get used to those appealing crow's feet at the edges of his eyes. She snorted a damp chuckle. "My dad taught me to play basketball. We'd shoot a few hoops almost every day, until…" She shook her head. "Never mind. It's a good memory. I hang on to those."

"Me, too." His gaze held heart-deep understanding. "I have lots of great memories of fifteen years with my wife. She passed away three years ago. Cancer."

"I'm so sorry."

He shrugged and cocked his head. "Life goes on, as we both know."

Nicole looked away. Maybe the fellowship of shared loss was part of this man's attraction for her. She could use a kindred spirit for a friend. Too bad this kindred spirit was also investigating a crime that implicated her last living close relative.

"I'd like to have more good memories with my grandmother. If what little I can say will help catch her attacker, I'll tell." She shared her grandmother's frantic bedroom search after the discovery of the baby's remains and the odd incident with the garbage.

Rich scratched the side of his neck. "So you think your grandmother might have disposed of something pertinent to the investigation?"

"I can only tell you what I observed…and what I didn't observe. What happened to that garbage bag? I know there's been a series of thefts in the area, but I hardly think the culprits are digging through the trash for valuables."

Rich's gaze narrowed on the opposite wall as if drilling for clues in the paint. "Apparently someone is."

Nicole spread her hands. "But if they found what they wanted in the garbage bag, why did they come after my grandmother? Obviously, she wasn't planning to tell anyone anything."

"Good question. Maybe they didn't want to take the chance that she would continue to keep silent. Or maybe they didn't find what they were looking for and returned to search. Maybe they still haven't found it."

"In other words, they could come back?"

Rich nodded. "You might want to stay somewhere else until this case is solved."

Nicole's insides churned. "I won't be driven from our family's home. I'm the only one left to protect it. Besides, I don't have anywhere else to go." Rich opened his mouth, but she lifted a hand. "I'll have an alarm system installed. Grandma will squawk like a ruffled chicken when she finds out, but I'll do it anyway."

Her gaze fell to her toes, and her stomach, too. *Please, God!* If only her grandmother would live to complain.

A squeaky shoe tread brought both of their heads around. Dr. Mead entered the waiting area, expression grim. She stopped in front of their chairs. Nicole's heart tried to pound right out of her rib cage.

"It's a good thing Jan Keller has a hard head," the doctor said.

"She's alive?" Nicole clasped her hands together.

"Is she awake?" Rich stood up.

The doctor shook her head. "Better for her that she's not right now. She has a skull fracture and a grade-four concussion with evidence of subdural hematoma."

"She's bleeding in the brain," Nicole said.

"Correct," Dr. Mead confirmed. "And for your information," she switched her gaze to Rich, "there are no other signs of a struggle on her body—no bruising and nothing under her fingernails."

Rich got busy with his pen and notebook. "So the assailant took her by surprise?"

"Not necessarily. The shape of the head wound suggests that she was facing her attacker."

Nicole gripped the arms of her chair. "She knew who hit her? Maybe let him in?"

"Not necessarily." Rich closed his notebook. "She might have been startled by an intruder, whirled to face him, and then been struck. That's one of the many questions she can answer when she wakes up."

Dr. Mead narrowed her eyes. "Even if Jan wakes up with all her faculties, she may not remember the events surrounding the attack. Amnesia related to head trauma is common."

Nicole rose. "You said *if* she wakes up."

The doctor's compassionate gaze sent a shiver to Nicole's middle. She'd seen that look of helpless sympathy directed toward her too often in her lifetime.

"I wish I could make promises," Dr. Mead said, "but I can't. Her prognosis is shaky at best. We need to helicopter her to the severe head trauma unit in the Twin Cities. The chopper is on the way. Unfortunately, there won't be room for you in the bird. You'll have to drive."

Nicole bit her lip. The road trip would consume over three hours.

"I'll chauffeur you, cop speed," Rich said.

"Let's go then." She leaped up. "I don't want to waste a minute."

On the way to her grandmother's house to collect a few things, Nicole clutched her oversize purse like a shield on her lap. Scary how at home she felt in the front seat of a police vehicle. You'd think she'd hate everything to do with the occupation.

She wasn't under any illusions about the offer to follow the chopper to the Cities. Rich wasn't being a Good Samaritan. He was still hoping for lucid words from the patient that would help him solve his case. Even so, accepting the ride was to her advantage. A police car could reach the major hospital far more quickly than a civilian vehicle following the speed limit.

Then why did she feel like she needed to protect herself? One glance at Rich's strong profile gave her the answer. Even in this moment of extreme stress, she found the police chief way too appealing for the safety of her broken heart.

SIX

"Do you have new plans for the sewing shop?" Rich glanced at the set profile of his passenger as he guided the police SUV up Highway 7 toward Minneapolis. Nicole barely batted an eyelash in response. "I mean, since you've been cleaning things out, I just wondered if you were making room for something."

"Huh?" Her head swiveled his direction. "I'm sorry. I was a million miles away."

"At least 120 miles anyway."

She gave a tired grimace. "What did you ask me?"

"Just curious about your plans for the shop."

"If my grandmother has her way, it'll be same old, same old, and that won't cut it in today's economy."

"But…" Rich prompted.

"I want to go into machine embroidery." Enthusiasm touched Nicole's expression. "There's a growing market for custom embroidered shirts, blanket throws and team apparel. The shop could turn a profit. I've studied the demographics, and we'd be the only supplier in the county."

"You've done your homework."

The light on Nicole's face faded. "Grandma thinks I'm just grasping at straws to keep busy while I grieve. She's afraid the machinery will keep her customers away in droves, when I believe the products would draw new customers from younger generations. My degree is in business administration, and I've thought this through. Grandma doesn't want to face it, but her current clientele is petering out. They're either going to the nursing home or..." She shook her head.

"Change can be difficult for the elderly." Rich nodded. "My grandmother had to be dragged practically kicking and screaming into the retirement village she thoroughly loves now."

Nicole chuckled. "I know Grandma would actually enjoy making the embroidered products if she'd give the idea a chance." She halted and blinked rapidly.

Rich looked away, respecting Nicole's emotional space. She had to be wondering if her grandmother would have the opportunity to try a new thing. This lady impressed him more every time he talked to her. He hadn't known she had a college degree.

"So what about you?" Her light tone was forced. "I checked in the phone book, and there are no other

Hendricks families in Ellington. Where are you from?"

"Grew up on a farm about an hour away from Ellington. There weren't any other Hendricks families there, either. Holidays were quiet. Sure enjoyed Big Stone Lake though."

Nicole shuddered and let out a small laugh. "It's a big lake, for sure. I nearly drowned in it once. I was seven and my parents and grandparents took me on a picnic in a park there."

"Really?" Rich shot her a strong look. "That must have been scary."

"I ventured outside the marked boundaries of the swimming area and tumbled over an unexpected drop-off. I was sure my days were over. Then this bigger boy grabbed me by the hair and hauled me to the surface."

"Wow! Your folks must've been happy with that kid."

Nicole shrugged. "I don't think they got to meet him. I was bawling and screaming and choking so bad, my grandpa swooped me out of the boy's arms. By the time they got me calmed down so I could tell them what happened, the boy was gone."

Rich's throat tightened. It couldn't be! But maybe... "Were you wearing a blue one-piece swimsuit with a yellow starfish on it?"

Nicole gaped at him. "You're a good cop, but

don't tell me you found that out on a background check."

"When I was a young teenager, I hauled this dark-haired little girl out of the drink and didn't get her quite onto the shore when this big guy grabbed her from me and knocked me down. I think he thought I was hurting you. I was pretty scared myself and ran off."

"You're kidding!" Nicole's brown eyes popped wide. "If that was me, I had no idea Grandpa hit you."

Rich laughed. "Well, if my granddaughter was howling and kicking and clawing in some stranger's arms, I'd do the same thing."

"Clawing?"

He rubbed his right arm. "Still have a couple of scars on my forearm. I don't think you liked having your hair pulled, and boy, did you have fingernails."

Nicole pressed her hands to her chest. "I can hardly believe it! You saved my life, got scratched and beaten up for your efforts, and now, here we are, grown up and driving down the road together. That's got to be more than a coincidence." She gazed at him with deep warm eyes. "It's my opportunity to say what should have been said then. Thank you soooo much! If Grandpa were here, he'd shake your hand and slap you on the back so hard your teeth would rattle."

Rich grinned and shook his head. "I'll pass. He already made my teeth rattle once." He rubbed his jaw.

Nicole's soft giggle did crazy wonderful things to Rich's insides. So did the memory of her Grandpa Frank's right hook. He had proven capable of violence back then, but Rich would think less of the man if he hadn't been quick to defend his granddaughter, even if it was a misunderstanding. If Frank was involved in the death of the baby in his backyard, maybe what happened was an accident. Could the Kellers have kidnapped Samuel for the money, fully intending to return him, but then the child died, and they had to bury him instead?

The dispatcher's voice came over his radio, jerking Rich out of speculation. He answered the call.

"Hey, Chief," the day dispatcher greeted him. "You wanted to be informed of any developments in the rose garden baby case. The medical examiner and the forensics tech agree that cause of death on the child was a broken spine. They say the injuries are consistent with shaken baby syndrome."

Nicole's face went ashen. Rich opened his mouth to chew on the dispatcher for talking case details with a civilian on board, but Nicole stopped him with a hand on his arm.

"It's okay," she said. "You know I'll keep it under my hat. Besides, now I'm beyond sure that my grandparents had nothing to do with that baby's death. They would never shake a child. Never!"

Rich lifted an eyebrow. But Grandpa would punch a teenager. He thanked the dispatcher and replaced the radio in its holder. "If so, that leaves us at square one with loads of questions."

"Maybe not." Nicole angled toward him. "The most common culprit in shaken baby syndrome is a parent or a family member."

"Are you suggesting someone in the Elling family killed the precious heir?"

Nicole crossed her arms and turned away. "I'm merely going with statistics."

Rich stifled the impulse to tell her that he fully intended to put the Ellings under a microscope. It wouldn't be professional to discuss the direction of his investigation with a civilian, particularly someone related to a suspect. But her remark might bear more weight than she knew. If Samuel's death was caused by someone in that household, he wouldn't put it past them to cover it up by staging a kidnapping. That scenario didn't explain how the child came to be buried in the Kellers' backyard, but it would be interesting to look into the Ellings' financial history to verify that the ransom was actually paid.

"Nice work," Rich let himself say. "You've given me some food for thought."

Nicole sniffed and dug inside her purse. She

pulled out the yellowed newspaper articles on the kidnapping.

"Why don't you read them out loud?" he said.

She shot him a questioning look. "You probably have this information memorized by now, plus a bunch of other stuff that wasn't released to the media."

"True, but a new pair of eyes can't hurt."

"Okay." She smiled. "I like a man who doesn't think he knows it all and can figure everything out by himself."

Rich's insides puddled. Appreciation of his investigative style was high praise from someone with her background.

She started reading the first article, written the day after Samuel Elling was reported missing. The journalism was a bit more dramatic and colloquial than current practice.

On the morning of November 5, 1957, Fern Elling stepped into her infant son Samuel's bedroom to find his crib empty. Her screams woke the household: Fern's father-in-law, Silas Elling, and his wife, Margaret, her husband, Simon, and her sister, Hannah. None of them reported seeing the child after he was put to bed the night before.

Within minutes, the estate crawled with law-enforcement personnel, but no trace of the child or an intruder was found. The next day, a ransom demand was received via telephone. The police have not released the details of the demand, and the family members have declined comment at this time.

The public is urged to report suspicious activity or strangers in the area to the local police department. A photo of Samuel accompanies this article. If the infant is spotted, report the matter to the authorities immediately.

The article continued with a reminder of the Ellings' prominent status in the area and a few lines of editorial-style sympathy toward the family. The piece concluded with a statement that the family was not receiving visitors and would not take phone calls from anyone other than the authorities or the kidnapper.

Nicole continued reading from one article to the next, but most simply regurgitated the original sketchy facts. Rich had to compliment his predecessors on keeping the activities of the investigation under their hats, though his study of the case records showed they were too surface for his taste in checking out the family members. Elling clout at work again.

"Here's a comment from the police chief at the time," Nicole said. "He says, 'We are exhausting every avenue of inquiry.' He doesn't come right out and accuse anyone, but the next line of the article goes on to mention that all of the Ellings' household staff has been dismissed, including a cook, a housekeeper and a groundsman."

She lowered the article. "Household staff are good suspects in a kidnapping, but obviously the investigation didn't reveal enough proof to make an arrest. Maybe the child's crying irritated a short-tempered kidnapper, and he reacted violently without thinking."

"Unless, of course, he meant to kill the child rather than return him."

"Terrible, but possible." Frowning, Nicole's gaze dropped. "Here's what Samuel's grandfather had to say. 'We will do whatever is necessary to recover the Elling namesake, and then we will employ any measure available to track down the child's abductor.'" She snorted. "The Elling namesake? The child? He talks about his grandson like he's a commodity, not a person."

"Typical of that family. Simon spouts the same rhetoric."

"I noticed."

"Figured you would. What do you think? Any hot leads pop out at you?"

She tugged her left earlobe. "Reinterviewing the household staff, if they're still alive."

"Okay. Good. Anything else?"

"And then the Ellings themselves. They're such a strange bunch."

"No argument there, but lack of familial feeling doesn't a murderer make."

Scowling, Nicole pulled another article out of the short stack. "There's one other thing. Here's an article written several weeks after Samuel's disappearance and after the ransom was paid with no result. Finally, the amount of the demand is printed—$5,718,000. Back then, that was an exorbitant amount, and it's an unusual number. Was there some personal significance in the figure to the kidnapper? Maybe the motive wasn't just greed. Maybe there's a vendetta here."

Rich let out a low whistle. "You think like a first-rate investigator. Maybe you missed your calling. It's not too late to follow in your dad's footsteps and take up a badge."

A chill radiated from the woman next to him. "I don't need that kind of stress in my life ever again, not in what I do for a living or who I let into my heart."

Rich's stomach went hollow. He realized at a young age that God made him to be a cop. If ever he remarried, his new wife would have to be on board with his life.

Nicole snuck a peak at the uniformed man seated in the chair across from her in the surgical ward waiting room. Rich stared at an open outdoorsman magazine, but he hadn't turned a page in a while. The guy was on the case while sitting still.

How amazing that Rich was the young teen who once rescued her from a watery death. Was some subconscious recognition behind the attraction she felt for him? If so, hopefully it would wear off now that she knew the reason for it.

Nicole fidgeted with her purse strap. Grandma Jan had survived the flight, thankfully, and was now in surgery to relieve the pressure on her brain and remove a bone chip. An hour had crawled past with no fresh word.

Rich laid the magazine down on a side table. "I'm going to grab a cup of coffee and check in with the office back home. Do you want anything?"

My grandmother awake and all right. She shook her head, and Rich left. Her gaze followed his long-legged stride, and her heart did a two-step. If this attraction was going to wane, the process wasn't off to a good start.

Time to get her mind off a certain charismatic cop and worries for her grandmother. Neither preoccupation was productive. Nicole took her phone out of her purse. If she was forward enough to voice suspicions about the Elling family, she ought to sniff around for something to back them up…or dispel them. How awful if the little guy was killed by someone in his own family.

After a brief Internet search, she found a site containing the history of the Ellington area. A few hundred years ago, that stretch of prairie was populated by nomadic bands of Native Americans. The area began to be occupied by nonnative settlers in the mid-1800s. In 1880, a railroad magnate by the name of Seth Elling bought up most of the farmland around a settlement that was later named after him.

Seth fancied himself a gentleman farmer and rented out a fair bit of his land to tenants, much like an English lord. The rest of the land was run by Seth's many sons. In fact, Seth wore out three wives to produce a dozen of them, as well as seven daughters. The man must have been obsessed with carrying on his name—an obsession that had clung through the generations. She read on in the historical narrative, sifting through a wide array of information to focus on the parts involving the Elling family.

The original Elling patriarch passed away in 1910, secure in his illusion that his legacy was ensured. Tragically, the influenza pandemic of 1918 wiped out all but a couple of daughters, and left only one son, Silas, the youngest. The once-thriving family tree had been pruned down to a few skimpy branches.

Silas's first wife suffered three miscarriages and then died in a drowning accident. Nicole lifted her eyebrows. How well was that "accident" investigated? His second wife produced two daughters in two years, then died in childbirth in the third year, along with the son she carried. *Okay, then. No suspicion of foul play there...unless you counted using a woman like a broodmare.* Disgust sat like a weight beneath Nicole's breastbone.

Finally, Silas's third wife, Margaret, earned her keep by giving birth to Simon. However, no more offspring came of the union. At least the woman didn't suffer any fishy accidents. No, Margaret lived to the ripe age of ninety-two, outlasting Silas by almost a decade.

What kind of woman did it take to hold her own with an Elling man? Another page in the narrative contained photos of the town of Ellington, as well as the founding family. Nicole enlarged the photo of Silas to the limit of her screen, and suppressed a shudder. Snakes had warmer eyes. The photo of Margaret answered Nicole's question. Her eyes were bookends of his. What sort of marriage did these two have? Nicole didn't bother to suppress this shudder.

Simon's marriage to Fern had endured to this day, and Fern was still alive. Rumor had it this latter detail was a surprise to most of the community. Fern had been at death's door too many times to count. Samuel had been their only son. If he'd lived, would he have turned out a cold-eyed, obsessed man like his forefathers?

Rich returned from his coffee mission with two

cups. He extended one toward Nicole. "I brought you some anyway."

Nicole accepted the offering. "Thanks." She blew on the steaming brew. "Do the Ellings still own most of the county?"

Rich settled into his earlier seat. "Over the years they've been whittled down to a few sections of land. None of the family actively farms anymore, so they rent out every square inch for crops or pasture. Some of their homestead sites are rentals, too, but some are vacant."

Nicole nodded. Decaying homesteads were a common sight in the rural areas as fewer families farmed larger pieces of land. Gone were the days of a farm family on every quarter. "Thanks for the thorough answer to my question."

"Why do you ask?"

Nicole pursed her lips. Should she give voice to a theory that had just occurred to her? She sipped at her coffee. Guess it couldn't hurt to bounce the idea off a pair of listening ears, especially when those ears were attached to the man who ran the investigation.

"The county should have a record of when the land sales occurred. I'm wondering if the Ellings had to sell off chunks in order to pay that enormous ransom."

"Okay. I follow you." Rich's gaze narrowed.

"Might be a strong indication that the ransom was actually paid."

"You think it might not have been?" Her heart lurched. "That the kidnapping was a put-on to cover up a worse crime?"

Rich cleared his throat and looked away.

Nicole laughed. He was cuter than ever when dismay struck. The cop in him hadn't wanted her to know the direction of his thoughts. "Your suspicions are safe with me."

Rich shot her a scowl, though his eyes smiled. "It's not a suspicion. More like a possibility to check out. But if that's not the direction you were going with your question, care to enlighten me?"

Nicole set her cup on a side table. "Selling off big chunks of land to pay the ransom probably sent the Ellings' finances into a tailspin. Maybe ruining the family financially was the point of the kidnapping. That makes the crime personal, not an impersonal act of greed."

Rich rubbed the back of his head. "Nice theory. Bears consideration. The Ellings have stepped on a lot of people over the years. The list of suspects could be legion."

"The attack on my grandmother narrows the field to someone local, as well as still alive." She hurried on in response to Rich's frown. "If the kidnapping was carried out by strangers, then the crooks would have had no need to stick around Ellington after they got the money. Therefore, they couldn't have responded so quickly to the discovery of the bones."

Rich sat forward and put his elbows on his knees. "You realize that if the assault on Jan is related to the infant's death, we have more reason than ever to suspect one or both of your grandparents was involved. Wouldn't you rather the attack turn out to be a random break-in?"

A wave of dizziness washed through Nicole's head, but she shook it away. "The truth needs to come out. I have to believe it will exonerate my family. Somebody somewhere is living a lie, and that's simply not my grandparents' character. Don't character witnesses count for something in a court of law?"

"Not as much as hard evidence."

"I'm betting you don't have much of that yet, or you'd have someone in custody."

Rich's solemn gaze locked with Nicole's as a chill gripped her marrow. That someone could turn out to be her grandmother. Was she prepared to face that outcome for the sake of truth and justice? But to live indefinitely under a cloud of doubt and suspicion, wouldn't that be many times worse?

SEVEN

"Jan Keller is in serious but stable condition."

The surgeon's words kept running through Nicole's head as she washed her face and hands at the hotel sink. How did she let Rich coax her into leaving the hospital and taking a hotel room, rather than bunking in a waiting room chair in case her grandmother took a turn one way or another? Dark bags under her eyes might be one reason. Sleep had been in short supply for a couple of days.

And then there was the rest of the doctor's message. "We need to keep her in a coma for a while—until the brain swelling goes down. Could be a week or more. Then we'll ease her off the medication and let her wake up in her own time."

In her own time? Nicole snickered as she dried her hands. Yes, Grandma Jan always did things in her own time and her own way.

The doctor had been noncommittal on a prognosis for full recovery. "We'll see what she's like when she wakes up," he said.

Nicole tossed the towel onto the counter. She'd have to live with that vague pronouncement. No one could promise anything, but waiting to find out was so hard. At least Grandma remained among the living. Nicole ran a brush through her tousled hair, and semi-tamed the thick waves that touched her shoulders.

There was one thing to look forward to this evening. Rich was going to pick her up shortly for a quiet meal out. He'd decided to get a room, too, rather than head straight back to Ellington. He planned to visit the MBCA office in the morning and pick the agents' brains about handling a cold case.

Nicole straightened her blouse and checked her clothing. Wrinkled, but it couldn't be helped. She'd only brought one extra set of street clothes, and that was for tomorrow. What did she care anyway? This wasn't a date, just a pair of acquaintances keeping each other company over a little necessary sustenance. The flutters in her tummy were merely the residue of worry over her grandmother. Of course they were.

A knock sounded on the door, and she clutched her middle. The butterflies had multiplied.

Nicole opened the door to find Rich standing in the hallway with his hands in the pockets of a pair of brown slacks. His striped shirt looked neat and crisp, and his grin sent Nicole's tummy butterflies into somersaults.

She cleared her throat. "You lost your uniform. Did you go shopping?"

Rich shuddered. "Me? Shopping?" He laughed. "If not for my daughter, I'd be a bum. I always keep a change of clothes in a zipper bag in the back of my unit."

"A prepared man." She was the one who resembled a bum—a sleep-deprived one at that. "Let me get my purse." Nicole retrieved it from the chest of drawers, and they proceeded up the hallway toward the elevator. "Don't forget our agreement to go Dutch."

Rich smiled. "I promise to rein in my gallantry."

She chuckled and some of her nervousness subsided. A few minutes later, they studied the menus in the hotel dining room.

Rich lowered his. "Here's my part of the supper pact. No shop talk. We give ourselves permission to relax."

"Deal." Nicole closed her menu and laid it on the table.

She glanced around the moderately busy restaurant. The decor featured paintings of colorful Victorian scenes and gingerbread trim on the woodwork. Savory smells had her salivating. When had she eaten last? Oh, yes. Early breakfast this morning with her grandmother—an aeon ago.

A waiter brought beverages and then took their orders. Rich began talking about his farm upbringing and had her laughing over anecdotes involving runaway cows and tractors stuck up to their axles in mud.

Their meals came, and Nicole spread her cloth napkin on her lap. "So why didn't you become a farmer?"

Rich pursed his lips as he cut his steak. "I liked the farm just fine. Great place to grow up. But farming was my brother's passion. I let him step into my dad's shoes. I always wanted to be a cop, so here I am."

Nicole sampled a bite of her garlic mashed potatoes. "My dad was that way, too. He lived for the badge. Never shirked when duty called."

"Hazard of the trade." Rich nodded. "But farming can be that way, too. Absorbing. Sometimes hard on family life."

"My mom coped pretty well. She was my role model when I married Glen. And I adored my dad. He was doing what he loved when he collapsed of a heart attack on duty. Too many donuts? Too many days and nights of burning the candle at both ends?" She shrugged. "I was a senior in high school. My mom never remarried, and then she was killed in a car accident a few years later."

"You've suffered a lot of loss over the years." His steady look searched hers.

Nicole dropped her gaze and sipped at her water. "You've had a big loss, too."

"My wife fought a good fight. I'm glad for those

final months we had together, even though they were rough with treatments and all. But then she went to a better place. I can be sad for me, but not for her."

Nicole studied him. Peace radiated from his eyes. "You mean that," she said. "A lot of people say those things, but it's a nice-sounding front for anger and unresolved grief." She laid her fork across her plate. "I know, because I'm still dealing with a lot of negative emotions. Not that I doubt where my loved ones are, but why did they go so soon? My dad never got to see me in my high school cap and gown, much less college. And he wasn't there to walk me down the aisle when I married a rookie cop straight out of the academy." Her hands fisted around the napkin in her lap. "Now Glen's gone, too."

She bit her lip and halted a further rush of words. *And I don't have his baby in my arms to leave me a piece of him. Why was that made impossible, too?*

Rich shook his head. "Doesn't make sense, does it?" His tone soothed.

Nicole let out a pent-up breath on a small laugh. "Here we are, supposed to be enjoying a relaxing evening, and I'm whining."

"That's all right. I'm honored you'd talk about these subjects with me."

She wrinkled her nose. "Thanks for not lecturing me to stop questioning and just have faith that God knows best."

Rich popped another bite of steak into his mouth

and chewed slowly. "I've never known faith and questions to be mutually exclusive. When we stop asking questions, we stop growing spiritually—or any other way."

A weight lifted from Nicole's chest. "Thanks. That's the most comforting thing anyone has said to me in a long time."

"My pleasure." He smiled. "Now, how about dessert after we finish this fine meal? My treat."

Supper ended on a positive note, with conversation returning to light topics. Then Rich insisted on walking Nicole to her door.

She laughed as they entered the elevator. "Your gallantry is getting away from you again."

He shrugged. "Not my gallantry so much as my cop-ness. I'd be protective of any beautiful woman wandering around an unfamiliar place at night in a big city."

Nicole sucked in a breath. He'd called her beautiful.

They arrived at Nicole's door. She looked up into Rich's eyes. Her light farewell words died on her tongue. His gaze was anything but detached. Her eyes widened. Would he try to kiss her? How would she react? Her heart did a little stutter-step.

Rich lifted his hand and brushed Nicole's cheek with his fingertips. Her eyelids drifted shut as if attached to his fingers by puppet strings. Warmth radiated across her skin. He was going to kiss her, and she was going to let him.

Breathless moments passed. Nothing happened.

Nicole opened her eyes. Rich's broad back was retreating up the hallway. A deep breath expanded her lungs. He hadn't kissed her. What a letdown, thank goodness! She wasn't herself right now. Her emotions were all over the place.

Assuring herself that she was indeed relieved over the missed kiss, she let herself into her room. Many guys would have taken advantage of a vulnerable female and stolen that kiss. Terry Bender's face darted past her mind's eye. Case in point. Just as well Rich was wise enough to keep his distance. He was the kind of man who played for keeps in the heart department, but nothing more than friendship could happen between them.

Nicole slipped into her pajamas and crawled between the sheets. Her weary body ached, and the wide mattress and soft pillows invited her to let tension fade into them. But her mind kept churning over thoughts about her grandmother, the baby's remains, Hannah and her disturbing Elling relatives, and then back to Rich.

And Glen.

She and Glen had wanted children in the worst way, but mere days before he was killed they got the news. Glen wasn't able to father a child. Nicole was willing to talk adoption. It didn't matter to her whether the baby was of their blood. He or she would become theirs through love. Glen wasn't ready for that option. Nicole figured if she gave him some space he'd work his way out of the funk and open his heart to a child who needed a family.

He never got the chance. Had his distraction about fatherhood contributed to him getting into the line of fire during the robbery?

Nicole rolled onto her side and punched her pillow. She'd never know. Tears wet the pillowcase, as they had too many nights to count. She still missed Glen far too much to consider another relationship, even if the sight of Rich did crazy things to her pulse.

Not only was Rich a cop, but he'd already raised his family. He had a grown daughter! It wouldn't be fair of Nicole to expect him to change his job and start over in the baby department. If and when she was ready for romance, Rich wasn't a candidate.

Back in uniform the next morning, Rich adjusted his gun belt around his hips then strode out the hotel room door. He wasn't as rested as he'd like to be, but then, current events hadn't exactly been conducive to a good night's sleep. If he was honest with himself, though, it wasn't the rose garden baby case that had disturbed his slumber, but a pair of wounded brown eyes.

Nicole was a long way from done grieving her husband. What had he expected? She'd take one look at him and realize she was ready to love again? Maybe he should reconsider his interest in her. She had a thing against cops as husband material. And there was something else bugging her, too. Something that was still too painful to talk about. What could be more devastating than the death of a loved one?

Rich arrived at Nicole's hotel room door and knocked.

"Who is it?" Her voice carried through the portal.

He identified himself. "Are you ready for me to take you back to the hospital before I go over to the forensics office?"

Silence answered for several heartbeats. "Not quite. You go on. I'll take a cab over."

Rich frowned. Was she really not ready, or had his affectionate touch on her cheek scared her away? He should have denied the impulse, but his fingers had seemed to possess a mind of their own. She hadn't pulled away. If anything, she'd looked ready for the next step. A kiss maybe? If this sudden avoidance was the aftermath of allowing a moment of contact, then it was a very good thing he hadn't pushed for more. Maybe he'd better not push her now, either—prove he wasn't a threat to the emotional space she needed.

"All right." The words left his lips reluctantly. "I'll stop by the hospital and check on you and your grandmother later today."

"Sounds good." The tone carried a wave of relief. Because he was leaving or because he was going to stop in at the hospital when he finished at the MBCA?

On the drive to the bureau headquarters in St. Paul, Rich got on the radio and checked in at the office. The dispatcher reported that a two-one-one had been called in early this morning. Rich groaned. Another robbery. The thefts seemed small potatoes compared to the assault on Jan Keller and the possibility that Nicole had uncovered the remains of Samuel Elling. But the persistent thefts of property were giving his department a black eye in the community.

"Hey, Chief." Terry got on the horn. "Let me call you on your cell."

Rich agreed. Must be something his deputy didn't want to discuss on the radio for the delectation of anyone with a police scanner. A few seconds later his cell played.

"Got an update on forensics from the Keller crime scenes," Terry said.

"Spill."

"The forensics tech headed back to his lab this morning with all the evidence from both the burial site and the attic. He says there are plenty of good fingerprints on the bat and the plastic bag that was used as a shroud. He won't have any idea who they belong to, though, until he gets a chance to analyze them with the proper equipment."

Rich huffed. "I expect some of the prints on the bat to come back to Jan and probably to her son, Nicole's father. The bat was his as a boy."

"Yeah, well, both those sets of prints will be in the system for elimination—Nicole's dad's because he was a cop, and Jan's because we just took 'em. Nicole's, too."

"Nicole's? You mean on the plastic bag."

"Or the bat. She called in the assault. Maybe Nicole and granny had an argument—something about that dead baby and—"

"Are you serious?" Rich's roar echoed in his own ears.

Terry's *gotcha* chuckle carried over the airwaves. "Not really. The motive for that extreme reaction is pretty flimsy. Unless there's something about this case we don't know."

"There are lots of blanks to fill in yet." Rich's words came out clipped, as he stuffed his eruption of anger down into his belly, where it smoldered and fumed like a banked volcano.

Why did he still let himself get blindsided by Terry's petty little jokes at his expense? Maybe because he was too infatuated with Nicole to think straight. That wasn't good. Not good at all as long as this case was on his docket.

"What's the scoop on this two-one-one last night?" Rich growled at his deputy.

"Dugan's Implement lost a half-dozen lawn

mowers and several skid loaders out of their storage shed in the back. The staff came in this morning to roll them out for display, but the padlock was cut and the shed had been cleaned out slick as a whistle."

"I thought Dugan's had an alarm system."

"On their showroom, yes, but the shed was for overstock and not wired."

Rich gusted a breath. "So it continues to look like we're dealing with clever amateurs. Smart enough to fly under the radar by not messing with alarms."

"Pickin's have been pretty good without tangling with alarms."

Too good. Rich's fume morphed into a boil. Those penny-ante crooks might think they were playing smart, but they'd mess up and get caught... eventually.

"Any leads?" he asked his deputy. "Tire tracks? Passersby notice unusual activity?"

"Nobody's come forward to say they saw anything suspicious last night, but we might have a partial tire tread from a trailer in the packed dirt near the shed. Of course, the tread could be from an innocent customer, too. Traffic is pretty regular in the lot."

Rich grunted. "Keep me updated on anything new. I'll be home by evening."

"Will do, Chief."

Rich tucked his phone away, scowling. His deputy was way too chipper for all the trash the department had on its plate. Probably because the guy was counting on inheriting Rich's badge after his boss got canned for incompetence. Rich squared his shoulders. Not going to happen. He'd better get a muzzle on these negative thoughts if he expected to nab the midnight larcenists, not to mention solve a half-century-old kidnapping and murder case.

Midafternoon, Rich left the headquarters of the MBCA with his head full of protocols on handling cold cases. He'd spent longer than he intended with the forensics experts, but it was worth the extra time to visit with the tech handling the evidence. The guy was a potent blend of sharp, level-headed and eager.

Already he'd determined that what had looked like dirt twined in the folds of cloth that wrapped the baby's remains was actually decayed rose petals. Another indication that whoever buried the child felt some sort of compassion or remorse, and unfortunately for Nicole, pointed even more strongly toward Frank and/or Jan Keller having played a part in the kidnapping—if indeed the remains were those of Samuel Elling. The tech also gave an educated opinion that the child had died and been buried within the time frame that the Elling baby was taken. He'd started the DNA testing for the bones and the hair from the brush Hannah had given Nicole. They'd soon know if Samuel had been discovered under the Kellers' rose bushes.

Rich returned to the hospital, a part of him a tad

too eager to lay eyes on Nicole again. Who knows how long she'd even tolerate his presence if the evidence forced him to slap cuffs on an old woman in a hospital bed. But why should it matter what she thought of him? He needed to forget Nicole. For now. Maybe forever.

Her voice carried to him as he neared Jan Keller's room, and his heart rate quickened. Was Jan awake? He knocked, and Nicole invited him in.

"Hi." He grinned at her.

She answered with a wan smile and closed the book on her lap.

His gaze darted to the figure on the bed. No, Jan wasn't awake. She lay still and pale, head wrapped in gauze and bandages. If not for the slow, steady beep of the heart monitor, it would be hard to tell she was alive.

"I was reading to her." Nicole lifted the book. "They say folks in a coma can hear what's going on around them. Did you have a good day?"

"Informative." And frustrating that there'd been another robbery. But she didn't need to know about that or the preliminary forensics results. "Would you like a ride back to Ellington?"

"Maybe I should stay here." Jan's hand lay outside the covers, and Nicole covered it with her own. "If she does have a shred of awareness, I want her to know that someone who loves her is nearby."

"Did you bring enough clothing to stay longer?"

Nicole shook her head. "I was in too much of a hurry to think that far ahead." She sighed. "I guess I'll go home with you now then turn around and drive my own car back here tomorrow."

Rich's heart leaped, but he shoved the rebellious organ back into place. A few more hours spent getting to know Nicole might turn out to be diabolical torture. Chances were that any hope of a relationship was doomed to disappointment.

The drive to Ellington passed too quickly. Nicole was easy to talk to, despite the heavy issues that lay between them. They'd continued their pact of the night before and kept the subjects light. The sun had sunk halfway below the horizon when they glided past the Cenex service station on the edge of town.

"Home, sweet home," Rich murmured, and Nicole answered with a smile. He didn't respond in kind. "I'm still not a hundred percent happy with leaving you alone in your grandmother's house."

"Worry wort. I'll be fine. I have a hunch that if Grandma's attacker was after something he either found it or discovered it wasn't there."

"As in, Jan told him she'd already destroyed it?" Nicole looked away.

He didn't voice the thought that hung in the air, thick as fog. Maybe once Jan Keller admitted she'd done away with evidence, the last thing that needed to be destroyed for the killer to feel safe was Jan herself.

"Can we stop by the shop quick?" Nicole asked. "I'd like to assure myself that everything's okay there."

"Can do."

Rich turned the SUV down Ellington's main street. Several century-and-a-half-old false fronts had been preserved among the downtown businesses, but most boasted updated facades of metal siding. The dollar store, the drugstore, the two banks, the hardware store and the newspaper and insurance offices slid past. All closed for the evening. The only restaurant on main street was also closed. Few cars sat on the tarmac and nobody trod the sidewalk. On the corner of the third block a cheerful wooden sign announced Jan's Sewing Room above a picture window displaying merchandise. Jan Keller's was among the buildings that possessed its original stone facade. Rich parallel parked his unit across the street, and he and Nicole got out.

Wind gusted at them and a candy wrapper skittered across the pavement in front of Rich's feet as they stepped toward the store. Nicole dug keys out of her purse. A slightly acrid smell teased Rich's nostrils as she stuck her key into the lock. Then a flicker caught his eye through the picture window.

"Don't!" he cried.

Too late.

Nicole pulled the portal wide, admitting a rush of wind to the building. A bass *whoom!* greeted the fresh air. Rich dived at Nicole and bore her to the sidewalk at the base of the stone front just as the picture window exploded above them and heat roared out.

EIGHT

Nicole stood huddled inside the emergency blanket draped across her shoulders as she watched red-gold flames consume her family's livelihood. Ellington Community Volunteer Firefighters darted here and there, spouting streams of water on the blaze and soaking neighboring buildings to prevent them from catching fire. Men's shouts rang in the deepening dusk. The crackle of flames and the wash of heat answered them. Nicole shivered despite the blanket and the balmy summer evening.

A few feet away, Rich sat on the end gate of an ambulance. His bloody and tattered uniform shirt had been discarded while EMTs tended to an assortment of glass cuts and small scorches on his broad back—injuries he had spared Nicole by covering her with himself. Naturally, he refused to leave the scene in favor of the hospital, even though he probably should have stitches.

"Thank you for saving my life," Nicole said for about the fourth or fifth time, but she couldn't stop reliving that horrible moment when Rich shoved her to the cement and spread himself atop her as fire boiled out at them. If not for taking instant cover behind the brick facade below the window, they would both be dead, rather than nursing minor cuts, scrapes and bruises. After the initial explosion, the fire had receded enough for the two of them to scuttle away and call for help.

Nicole rubbed an abrasion on her elbow. The raw flesh stung, but nothing like the fierce pain of witnessing the shop reduced to embers. Her gaze riveted on the blaze that was finally admitting defeat and dying before the determined efforts of the fire fighters. How had this happened?

"We'll find out."

Rich's stark statement drew Nicole's attention back to him. Had she spoken her question out loud, or was he reading her mind? Probably the latter. He was good at picking up on people's thoughts.

Rising, he gingerly shrugged into the shirt from their evening out in the Twin Cities. Shadows and light played over his grim features as evening darkness battled the reflection of ebbing flames. "We're going to get to the bottom of this. I promise."

Nicole nodded, throat too full to speak.

"Let me take you home now. I—"

"Chief!" The young officer, Derek Hanson, motioned to his boss.

Rich stepped away. Nicole trailed him, but she

doubted he noticed. His attention was fixed on a man holding a leash attached to a small dog. The man stood shifting from foot to foot next to the deputy.

Derek jerked a thumb at the man. "Paul here says he heard a couple of odd things a short while before you found the fire."

Found the fire? Nicole dropped the blanket from her shoulders and hugged it to her chest. Is that what Derek called nearly being blown into the next world?

"What can you tell us?" Rich shook Paul's proffered hand.

"Buster and I were out on our usual rounds—"

"Buster?"

Paul motioned toward the terrier that whined at the fire and hugged close to his master's legs. "When we got to the corner of the Sewing Room, I thought I heard glass breaking. I stopped and looked around, but didn't see anything. The street was deserted. Then I figured out the sound probably came from the alley around back."

"Did you investigate?"

Paul stiffened. "Are you kidding? I—er, well, that isn't Buster's and my usual route, so we moved along up main street. A couple seconds later, I heard an engine roar, like someone was giving it the gas."

"Did you see a vehicle?"

"Nope. The car noise came from the alley, and it went the opposite direction."

Rich's quick sigh echoed Nicole's. She continued to hang back and let Rich handle the questions. This was his job, and he did it well.

"Thanks for the info, Paul," Rich said. "One more question. Was there anything distinctive about the engine sound?"

Paul scratched under his ear. "Deep. Kind of gravelly like a sports car."

Rich and Derek exchanged glances. Nicole knew a couple of people with sports cars right in the Kellers' neighborhood. Did the information mean something special to the police?

"You know who to check up on," Rich told his deputy.

The younger man jerked a nod.

"You done with me?" asked the man with the dog.

"Thanks, Frank." Rich shook his hand again, and Buster and his master hustled away.

Derek pulled a frown as his gaze followed man and dog. "Too much crazy stuff happening around here these days. I thought I'd come back home after the academy and cut my rookie teeth in a quiet little town. Hah! The equipment thefts with no clues and no witnesses are downright freaky. Makes us look stupid. Then a baby is discovered beneath an upstanding citizen's rose garden, an old lady gets attacked in her home and now this."

"Hang in there," Rich said. "We'll catch these

perps. They'll make a mistake, and then they'll be behind bars before they know what hit them."

"I sure hope you're right. Anything developing on the rose garden baby case?"

"I've got a few angles to pursue. I want to find out who might have had a vendetta against the Elling family. Business associates. Employees."

Derek grimaced. "My grandmother, Gudron Hanson, was a cook for the Ellings at the time of the kidnapping. My mom told me about it, but warned me not to bring the subject up to her. The incident broke Grandma Goody's heart, but not because she lost her job. Mom says Grandma was going to quit anyway because she was about to marry my grandfather."

Nicole caught her breath and stepped closer.

"Is your grandmother still alive?" Rich asked the question uppermost in Nicole's mind.

"Sure," Derek said, "but she's in the nursing home and not all there, if you know what I mean. Even if she wasn't going in and out of focus like some water-logged camera, she won't talk about the kidnapping. My mom said she'd just look sad and walk away if anyone mentioned it."

"I'm going to try talking to her anyway tomorrow," Rich said. "You follow up on that sports car while I take Nicole home, I—" Rich turned and nearly ran into her.

Nicole gazed into his startled face. "When you talk to Goody tomorrow, I want to be there."

"I don't think—"

"Good idea!" the deputy burst out. "She might open up to you, Nicole. She thought the world and all of Jan Keller. Used to be a regular customer at the sewing shop."

Nicole nodded. "I remember my grandma mentioning her friend Goody Hanson."

Derek looked toward his boss. "If you're set on talking to her, I figure she'd talk to a woman before some strange man. No offense, Chief."

Rich frowned and studied Nicole. "Wouldn't you rather stay home so you can look for the insurance information on the shop?"

"The policy will wait where it is until I get around to finding it."

Rich lifted his hands in defeat. "All right. I'll pick you up in the morning. But now let's get you home, unless you can think of some place else to stay."

"Negative."

"I thought not." Rich poked a finger at Derek. "Pass the word. Drive-bys on the Keller property every half hour."

"Got it!" Derek trotted away.

Rich ushered Nicole toward his SUV with a hand at the small of her back. Sweat popped out on

Nicole's forehead as she fought an overwhelming impulse to lean into his comfort and let him wrap an arm around her. Brooding silence hung between them in the vehicle on the short drive to the Keller home. Rich must have a million better things to do than chauffeur her around, but he did it without complaint. He walked her up to her door, and insisted on checking the inside of the house. The place was deserted, and the mess was exactly as it had been only yesterday before their hasty run to the Twin Cities hospital.

"I'm sorry...about everything." Rich squeezed her hand at the door as she let him out.

"I know." She pulled her hand away. The warmth of his touch was too appealing to her emotions, his broad shoulder too inviting for a good long cry.

And then he was gone.

Numb and exhausted, Nicole locked the door then checked every bolt on every entrance and window. Finally, she dragged herself upstairs to her grandmother's guest bedroom where she'd installed her things. Not much to show for a decade of married life, and before that, full and active growing up years. Most of her belongings were in storage. Not needed here at Grandma Jan's.

What if her grandmother never came back? With the shop gone, there'd be nothing to hold Nicole in

Ellington. Where would she go? It seemed no matter where she tried to plant roots, they got torn up.

Nicole shook herself. She couldn't afford to spend time feeling sorry for herself. The important thing was to catch whoever assaulted her grandmother. Had that person also torched the shop? Or had that been an accident? Maybe a gas line had sprung a leak.

Sure, just like Grandma was attacked by a passing burglar who had nothing to do with the baby in the rose garden.

Her teeth ground together. Somebody had a lot to answer for, and they weren't driving her out of the family home until and unless she was ready to leave. There was one item from her married life that she'd brought here. Something her grandmother knew nothing about because she would have had a "conniption," as she'd put it.

Nicole got her suitcase out of the walk-in closet and plunked it onto the bed. From a zipper compartment in the bottom she pulled a shiny black object. The weight was heavy in her hand. She hadn't kept the pistol Glen had bought her loaded and in her dresser drawer since moving to Ellington. Time to revert to that old cop's wife's habit.

If this creep came skulking around here again, he'd have far more to deal with than one little old lady. Nicole was a crack shot on the firing range, but she'd never pointed a gun at a human being. In this case, she wouldn't hesitate.

Would she?

The next morning, Rich scowled at the road on the five-minute drive from the Keller house to the nursing home on the east edge of town. The faint scent of smoke tainted the atmosphere, reminding him of last evening's tragedy. Plus the dispatcher had called at 7:00 a.m. to tell him a farmer had reported small equipment missing overnight. Then Nicole had answered his knock around eight-thirty looking too cute for his comfort, despite the dark circles under her eyes. He'd noticed the same smudges on his own face while shaving this morning. They were a fine pair of raccoons off to interview a befuddled octogenarian.

"Are you in pain?"

Nicole's soft query jerked him out of his dark meditations.

"A little." He rippled his shoulders and winced. "No worse than high school."

"High school?"

"We beat each other up pretty good in football." A smile tugged at his lips.

She laughed. "All in the name of becoming a hometown hero. You did it right in my books last night."

Little ripples of pleasure passed through Rich then

the glow of the compliment dimmed. "I just wish it hadn't been necessary."

"Me, too."

Comfortable silence fell as Rich found a parking space in the small lot. They got out and headed for the front door of the single-story, redbrick building.

Nicole cast him a questioning look. "How much do you want me to participate in the conversation?"

Rich smiled at her. She was a savvy woman and thinking clearly, despite her losses. "If Goody responds better to a woman, maybe you could get her talking and relaxed."

"Before you spring the bomb on her."

Rich winced. "It's not to my taste to sneak up on an old woman, but we've got to pursue every lead we can get, even if it's a long shot."

"I wasn't criticizing. I totally get it. As crazy as it sounds, Derek's grandmother is a potential suspect in the baby case."

Rich opened the door for Nicole, and they stepped into a spacious lobby/dining room combo. An ornate fountain bubbled in one corner and a sitting area featured leather furniture and a large-screen TV. The couch stood empty, but several residents watched a game show from their wheelchairs. The large space smelled of whatever had been served for breakfast. Rich's stomach growled, and he cleared his throat to cover the sound. After he got the call about the missing equipment, he'd forgotten to eat.

Fortunately, Nicole had gone ahead to the reception desk to ask where to find Gudron Hanson. Soon they were in a room about the size of a generous bedroom. The area held a dresser, a single bed, a television and stand, a shelf hosting several live plants, an enormous bulletin board crammed with family photos, a straight-backed chair and a large recliner. Goody, garbed in a flowered housedress, reigned over her room from the recliner. Wispy white hair framed a broad Nordic face seamed with wrinkles.

Milky-blue eyes gazed in their direction "Wh-who is it?" she quavered.

"Nicole Keller," Nicole answered, using her maiden name. "And my friend Rich Hendricks."

"Hendricks?" The old woman frowned up at him. "Don't know any Hendricks. Know some Kellers." Her gaze fell to Nicole. "You related to Frank and Jan?"

Nicole settled on the guest chair with a chuckle. "I'm their granddaughter."

A smile spread across Goody's face, exposing teeth too perfect to be her own. "How nice you came to visit. How are your grandparents? Oooh, I forgot. Frank passed, didn't he?"

"That's right, but Grandma Jan's still kicking." Nicole's face paled, but her voice remained steady.

Rich mentally applauded her composure despite the thoughts and fears that had to be going through her mind. He squeezed her shoulder, and she sent him a grateful glance. She was doing great, and Derek's grandmother seemed more aware than he'd expected. Maybe something useful could come from this interview after all.

For the next few minutes, Nicole and Goody ignored him as they reminisced about Jan and Frank Keller. The old woman's delighted cackle punctuated the conversation. A sparkle lit Nicole's gaze at the fond memories. Rich bit back his questions. These women deserved a few lighthearted minutes. He could be patient.

Goody squinted up at him. "You this young lady's beau, big fella?"

Heat licked Rich's cheeks, and Nicole's face crimsoned.

"Like she said, I'm a friend," he answered.

The old woman looked him up and down. "You're wearing some sort of uniform. Can't quite make it out. Are you a soldier?"

"Police officer."

Goody's eyes widened then she grinned. "You know my grandson, Derek? He's a policeman, too."

"This is Derek's boss," Nicole inserted. "Rich is the chief here in Ellington."

The old woman narrowed her eyes. "What happened to Chief Wilson?"

"He retired, ma'am," Rich said.

Goody's wrinkles folded in on themselves. "Can't count on nothin' staying the same."

Nicole covered the octogenarian's hand with her own. "You've been through a lot of changes, haven't you, Goody?"

"Sure have." The woman bobbed her head. "More'n I care to say. More than I remember even. The old noggin' ain't what it used to be." She tapped her head with a forefinger.

The opening wasn't going to get any better. Rich stepped closer.

"Your grandson's a good cop. He mentioned that you used to work for the Ellings."

Goody went stiff. "Long time ago. Not my best memories. Doesn't matter now."

"Unfortunately, the past must be discussed."

Nicole fidgeted with her purse strap while Rich told Goody about finding a baby's bones in the Kellers' yard and the attack on Jan Keller. He left out the explosion at the shop. That was more information than Goody needed and could possibly end up attributed to natural causes. *Sure. Just like Jan Keller's attacker was a common burglar.*

As he talked, all animation faded from Goody's face. Soon tears formed ragged trails down her furrowed cheeks.

"Wicked doings," she muttered. "They broke the sixth one."

The sixth one of what? Nicole's head jerked up. "Who did wicked things? My grandparents?"

The woman shook her head. "Not them. It was them!"

"Them who?" Nicole leaned forward and gripped the arm of Goody's chair.

"What can you tell me about Samuel Elling's kidnapping?" Rich jumped in. This conversation needed solid direction.

Goody's head swayed back and forth, and she wrung age-spotted hands.

"You worked in the Elling home at the time," Rich pressed. "The help always knows more than the family thinks they do."

"Please, Goody!" Nicole burst out. "We need to catch whoever is hurting people now in order to hide what they did."

The old woman covered her ears with her hands. "Accursed seed! Legacy of lies!" Her voice grew shrill.

Nicole sent Rich a helpless glance and half rose from her seat. Goody's hand shot out like a bird's talons and gripped Nicole's wrist. "Secretssssss. Those poor women!"

"Who do you mean, Goody?" Nicole leaned close, but the older woman stared around, eyes wild.

"Nobody kno-o-ows!" She wailed, fit to wake the dead.

A nurse rushed into the room. "It's all right,

Goody." The woman motioned to Rich and Nicole. "You'd better leave. She goes along great for quite a while then something sets her off, and she has one of her spells. Best thing is dark and quiet." The nurse pulled the curtains.

Pale and wide-eyed, Nicole headed for the door, and Rich followed on reluctant feet. There was more to Goody's outburst than just "a spell." Somewhere in the wild nonsense lurked a thread of sense. But how could he pick it out through the knotted mess?

NINE

As she hurried out of the nursing home beside Rich, Nicole's skin crawled as if tiny bugs scampered across her flesh. What a frightening reaction from an otherwise sane-seeming woman. Sure, Goody had been a little vague at times, but she'd been sharp as a tack about bygone days. Then again, if she'd worked for any length of time in the Elling household, particularly at the time of the kidnapping, that would be enough to give anyone the willies.

They reached the fresh air and sunshine of the outdoors, and Nicole took a cleansing breath. "Goody knows something about the Ellings, but it may not have anything to do with the kidnapping."

Rich shot her a hard look. "Why do you say that?"

They reached his SUV, and Nicole met his gaze across the hood. "She mentioned 'those poor women.' I think she meant the Elling women. I've researched the family, and the Elling wives have had it tough."

Rich shrugged. "I'm sure Fern, Margaret and Hannah were pretty broken up about Samuel's disappearance. Goody probably witnessed a lot of weeping and wailing."

Nicole pursed her lips and shook her head as she climbed into the vehicle. She didn't have enough information to argue with him, and she could be wrong, but she had the sense that Goody referred to a pervasive horror in that household.

Rich pulled out of the parking lot, gnawing on one side of his lower lip, gaze distant. The man was thinking anyway.

Nicole rubbed her palms against her jeans, quashing the jitters. "It feels a little like déjà vu to ask, but could we stop downtown? I'd like to get a look at what's left of the shop by daylight."

Rich headed the SUV toward the heart of Ellington. "I was on my way there anyway after I dropped you off back home. The investigator from the State Fire Marshall's office should be sifting through the debris this morning. Maybe he can give us some idea how the blaze started."

The charred and blackened stone front of the shop still stood, but the wood structure behind it was pretty much gone. Heart leaden, Nicole inhaled a lungful of acrid air. A lifetime of work put into this business, now reduced to wet ashes. How would she break this news to her grandmother? Provided she had that opportunity. Her call to the hospital this morning had yielded no encouragement—no particular discouragement, either. Jan Keller remained unconscious in serious but stable condition.

A gray-haired man in jeans, a sports shirt and a feed cap wandered around the shop's remains, studying the gutted structure. He was dressed pretty casually for a state official. A reporter? She wasn't ready to talk to one of those.

"Stan!" Rich called to the guy.

He waved and meandered over to them, craggy face unsmiling. "Hey, Rich. Too much excitement around here."

"I'll say." Rich grunted. "Stan, this is Nicole Mattson, the owner's granddaughter. Nicole, this is Stan Bolton of the fire marshall's office."

Nicole shook Stan's meaty hand. "Any idea how this happened?"

Stan darted a glance toward Rich and then returned his gaze to Nicole. Was there some kind of cop/fire official secret communication going on?

"I have a right to know," Nicole pressed. "My grandmother is incapacitated, and I'm handling her affairs."

"It's okay." Rich nodded toward Stan.

Nicole suppressed a spike of resentment at the need for a third-party go-between in order to gain a little cooperation.

"Honestly?" Stan glanced at the charred remains. "It's too soon to be sure about the cause of the blaze.

I'd rule out a gas leak. The explosion would have been much more powerful, and there is no telltale odor."

Rich nodded. "From what I observed when we stood at the door, the blaze started in the back room. That's where I saw the flicker of flames."

"Good to know." Stan took his cap off and wiped his brow with the back of his arm. "Assuming that's our point of origin, I'll start sifting through the debris at the back of the store." He sent a sympathetic smile toward Nicole. "Chances are we'll discover a wiring malfunction. In these old properties it's the most common cause of fire."

"Thank you," Nicole said. "I'd appreciate being informed as soon as you know anything."

"I'll give a full report to Rich when I have it. He'll pass the info along to you and the insurance company." Stan touched the bill of his cap and walked away.

Nicole's stomach roiled. She wanted answers, and she wanted them now. But she didn't want them filtered through the police. Sure, she trusted Rich, but if something criminal was uncovered, his professional duty might constrain him from telling her the whole story.

"Do you want to go to the courthouse with me?"

"What?" The meaning of Rich's words didn't register. "The courthouse? I— Oh, you mean to check and see when the Elling land sales occurred?"

He awarded her a half smile. "You did want to look into that angle, didn't you? It's public record, so we might as well do it together, rather than putting the office staff to the trouble twice."

Nicole spurted a laugh. "By all means. I like a public servant who's concerned about saving taxpayer time and money. Then I do actually need to get back home and hunt up that insurance information."

"Yes, ma'am." He led the way toward his vehicle. "You'll have to buy me a chauffeur's chapeau one of these days."

She chuckled. "I've about forgotten what it's like to drive my own car. I'd intended to return to my grand-mother's bedside today, but as long as she's stable, I'd better stick around here and handle matters."

They climbed into the SUV, and Rich sent her a grave look. "I'm so sorry you're having to deal with all of this unpleasantness."

"It's hardly your fault."

"But it's on my watch, and I'll follow the evi-dence and turn over every rock until the truth comes out."

Nicole's heart squeezed. "I would expect no less. That baby deserves justice. So does my grandmother. Neither you nor I had anything to do with what hap-pened back then. All we can do is make sure the right things are done in the here and now." Her throat thickened, but she forced out the words. "Whatever the cost."

"You're a brave woman."

Rich's admiring look warmed Nicole's insides. He was wrong though. She wasn't brave. She was petrified and feeling very alone.

"Glen was a lucky man," he added.

Tears pulsed behind Nicole's eyes. "Thanks." She blinked rapidly and pressed her fingertips against her cheekbones. Rich seemed not to notice her near breakdown, and she mentally thanked him for that kindness also.

A half hour later, they trod down the courthouse steps with copies of all the land transactions done by the Ellings in the past sixty years. Sure enough, a spate of sales took place at the time of the kidnapping.

"Unfortunately," Rich said as they got on the road, "the sales were to a variety of local people, not one person or entity."

"Which reduces the probability that the kidnapper's true motive was to get the Elling land and collect the ransom to reimburse themselves at the same time."

Rich grinned at her. "You don't like it when I say so, but you think like a cop."

When he smiled at her that way, Nicole couldn't muster a spark of resentment for the comparison. The guy was seriously too cute for his own good—er, her own good. She stared out her passenger-side window. They had entered her neighborhood. The Keller home lay ahead, outwardly the same as the one she'd known all her life, but changed forever inside of Nicole because of all that had happened in the last few days.

Rich pulled up outside the house.

Nicole put her hand on the door latch, but didn't get out. "There's one other theory that gets shot in the foot."

Rich made a humming noise. He knew, but she had to say it—get it out in the open, rather than leaving the knowledge hang like a guillotine blade over their heads.

"If the Ellings paid the ransom, there goes the notion that they staged the kidnapping to cover for someone among them who shook that poor infant. That puts us right back looking for a person or persons with greed as a motive." She clamped her lips shut.

Grandma was well fixed. All their property was paid for. Nicole had always assumed their financial well-being was because Grandpa Frank had such a good job as a bank president. What if she looked back in their financial records and discovered that the payoffs occurred around the time of the kidnapping?

Her heart bumped to a halt then leaped into over-
drive. Rich had taken the financial records from the
shop. What would they reveal?

Now what lit a fire under Nicole? Rich frowned as
she hustled, stiff-legged, up her front walk, digging
in her purse for her keys. At the door she turned
and waved, her smile a bitter grimace, not a fond
farewell. He shouldn't have made that remark about
her thinking like a cop.

Sighing, Rich pulled away from the Keller residence and headed back downtown toward the restaurant. As his grandfather used to say, his stomach
was beginning to think his throat had been cut. He
walked into the café, and conversation dimmed then
died, but not before he caught the Keller name on
people's lips. Several patrons called greetings, and
he responded in kind. Everyone knew better than
to ask him about the case, but that didn't keep the
hungry speculation from their eyes.

Conversation resumed as he took a seat at the
counter. Sure enough, the hot topics were last night's
fire and the discovery of the baby's remains in the
Kellers' backyard. Public sentiment seemed split
between support for the Kellers on the basis of
character versus suspicion based on circumstances.
Personally, he had to go with the character folks on
this one. For now. Mainly because he was coming
to know firsthand what an awesome granddaughter

the Kellers had participated in raising. Like that was objective criteria? Rich shook his head at himself. Well, in a sense it was, if he subtracted the romantic interest.

"What can I getcha today?" The waitress stopped in front of him, pad ready.

"Hey, Marty," Rich greeted her. The plump, gray-haired woman, part owner of the place, had been a fixture for as long as Rich had lived in Ellington. He ordered a Reuben sandwich with a side of potato salad and a cup of coffee.

Marty didn't bother to write on her pad. "The chief wants the usual," she hollered to the cook who stood peering over a high window shelf.

"Yo!" the guy responded with a thumbs-up.

Marty turned toward Rich. "One of these days you're gonna surprise me, but not today." She grinned and headed for the coffee station.

Terry plopped down on the swivel seat next to Rich just as Marty set his cup of coffee in front of him.

Rich took a sip without looking at his deputy. "What do we know about our most likely sports-car driver?" He kept his voice low.

"Tough break there. For us. Our favorite D.U.I. was M.I.A. yesterday. Didn't get home until late last night. He took Mommy Dearest shopping out of town."

"Shopping." Rich snorted. "What else is new?"

Of course, tracking down the unknown driver of an unseen sports car might be a waste of time if Stan concluded the fire started from natural causes. Rich's cell began to play, and he answered.

"You might want to get over here, pronto," Stan said. "I've got something to show you."

Rich's pulse leaped. "I'll be right there." He flipped his cell phone shut.

Terry eyed him with raised brows. "Need me for something?"

"Enjoy your lunch." He rose as his meal arrived. "Throw this in a to-go box for me, will you, Marty?"

The waitress rolled her eyes. "Like I said. One of these days you're going to surprise me."

A minute later, Rich tossed his lunch box into the passenger seat and drove up to the next block. He pulled into the alley behind the burned-out shop, where Stan stood waiting for him. Rich climbed out of his vehicle. As he approached, Stan held up a large baggie with some curved and soot-stained glass shards inside.

"And this means what?" Rich planted his hands on his hips.

"Molotov cocktail. Crude business with some gasoline and a lit rag stuffed inside a glass bottle. Whoever did this didn't care about making it look like an accident. They chucked it through a back window. Wouldn't have taken too long in this tinderbox to get a nice blaze going." He jerked his chin at the remains of the shop. "Then when you opened the door and gave the beast more oxygen—whoom!"

Rich accepted the evidence bag. "I'll have Derek process this for prints. He can scan any results and e-mail them to the forensics tech for evaluation."

"Sounds like a plan." The fire investigator rubbed the back of his neck. "I hate to see things like this."

"You and me both."

Someone had deliberately blown up Jan Keller's shop and nearly killed him and Nicole in the process. The timing of the incident—after business hours—indicated that property damage, not homicide, was the intention, but that didn't douse the burning anger in Rich's gut.

On the drive to the office, Rich replayed snippets of conversations he'd overheard at the restaurant. Had he caught echoes of fury in any particular voice? Nothing jumped out at him. Then again, too much jumped out at him. Judgmental words had been spoken by lots of different voices. Just as he'd feared. The location of the baby's bones invited confident, though unsupported, conclusions.

Surprising how high feeling still ran about that long-ago kidnapping. Had mob mentality spread enough to spur malicious action out of some misguided soul? He'd think less of this town if it had. Disturbing enough that some were siding against the

Kellers so quickly when Jan lay hovering between death and life, and her store had been destroyed. But then, the younger generation didn't know Jan well, or Frank at all. And the older generation suffered from the lingering effects of Elling dominance. He'd hate it if the evidence proved the gossips right.

Rich left the glass shards with Derek and wolfed down his cold lunch. He fielded a call from a reporter wanting a statement about the rose garden baby case and the shop fire, but all he gave was a no comment on ongoing cases. Then Terry came in from rounds, and Rich assigned him to cart the boxes of financial records from the sewing shop over to an impartial accountant in a neighboring town for evaluation.

After Terry left, grumbling about getting stuck with the dumb gopher jobs, Rich drove up to the Elling place. He no longer needed DNA from the baby's parents in order to confirm the child's identity, but he did still want to interview Fern. Surely she'd be available this time of day. He rang the bell and waited. A barefoot, rumple-haired Mason opened the door.

"All hail the chief." He sneered. "What do you want this time? Grandpa's not here and neither is my mom, and I didn't do anything, as I'm sure Deputy Dog has told you by now."

Rich reined in his temper. This kid was just fishing for a reaction. "I'm not here to see any of those people…or you. I'd like to speak to your grandmother."

Mason snickered and ran his fingers through his bed-head. "She's out cold. Took something for one of her migraines. Who knows when she'll grace us with her presence again. Could be suppertime, but probably not. I expect *Madame* will be served in her room."

At least Rich didn't have to feel like he was the only recipient of this punk's disrespect. Everyone was a candidate.

"So you and your grandmother and Hannah are the only ones home right now?"

"That'd be the size of it. If you want to talk to Hannah, she's in the garden. Probably sleeping on a bench. She doesn't do much actual gardening anymore."

Was that a hint of fondness in the young man's tone? Could be Hannah, in her vague way, had been the only one to show Mason much kindness when he was growing up.

"No, I don't need to speak to Hannah again. Thanks, anyway. I'll—"

"I know. You'll be back." The young man smirked.

"Tell your grandmother to call me."

Rich returned to his SUV. He looked up as he climbed into the vehicle, and that same curtain he'd noticed last time he was here twitched back into place. Rich's hands clenched around the steering wheel. Either Mason had lied to him about where everyone was and what they were doing, or else Fern or Hannah had awakened from their naps in time to spy out the window.

The Elling family had closed ranks on him. They were hiding something, but Rich didn't have a shred of hard evidence to wangle a search warrant, even from a sympathetic judge. As he drove away, Rich scowled into his rearview mirror at the brick mansion. Whether the Ellings wanted to believe it or not, he was going to uncover the secrets that mausoleum guarded.

Only one problem. How?

TEN

Nicole nibbled at a tuna sandwich without tasting it. The security company was booked solid and couldn't get to her job for a few days. Rich would have a fit… if she told him. Otherwise, except for a couple of interruptions from reporters calling for interviews that she declined, she'd spent the afternoon hunting for the elusive insurance policy to no avail. Surely, Grandma had insured the shop.

While Nicole looked, she'd put things in order from the police search, but had hardly made a dent. Amazing how easy it was to make a mess compared to the time it took to clean it up. Mostly, she'd concentrated on her grandmother's bedroom as the likely place to yield important papers. No insurance policy had come to light or anything to do with the baby buried in the backyard, but in the closet Nicole had found a wealth of photos from her dad's and her childhoods, plus a box of awards and school papers of her father's. Nicole discovered things she'd never known about her dad.

The sentimental journey had absorbed more hours than she should have allowed, but the distraction had been welcome. She would never have guessed her dad took dance lessons as a small boy or that he had a lead part in a play in junior high. An artsy streak wasn't what she associated with her manly-man father. The image was sort of jarring, like Clint Eastwood singing in the movie *Paint Your Wagon*. Come to think of it, that had been one of her dad's favorite old flicks. Now she knew why.

A knock sounded on the back door, and Nicole jerked. She laid the remnants of her sandwich on a plate and went to peer out the curtain over the door's window. Rich stood on the porch, gazing around as if searching for threats. She opened the door, and he stepped into the kitchen. His grim expression didn't convey comfort.

Nicole tensed. "Bad news?"

"Stan says the fire was arson."

A forlorn cry escaped her throat. "Who would want to burn the shop? Why? It can't be to destroy evidence. The place had already been searched."

"So had this house when someone attacked your grandmother."

Rich's bald statement sent a pang through Nicole. Maybe the motive was sheer malice. Who could possibly hate the Kellers so much? She couldn't recall her grandparents having a single enemy, unless she counted her grandmother's antipathy toward Hannah.

Was the feeling mutual? Hannah had shown herself plenty spry when she did that pirouette in her bedroom. Still, Nicole couldn't picture the plump, elderly woman tearing down those attic steps like the attacker had done or roaring around in a sports car setting fires. Of course, Nicole hadn't been able to picture her dad as a dancer or an actor, either, yet he'd been both.

"How did it happen?" Nicole steeled herself to absorb another vile report.

Rich described a crude Molotov cocktail flung through a back window.

"So anyone could have started the fire," Nicole said.

"That's about the size of it." Rich's gaze reflected the sad anger in Nicole's heart.

"Any leads on the driver of the sports car that the witness heard?"

Somber amusement flickered in Rich's eyes. "You know I can't tell you that."

"Of course not." Nicole sniffed. "But I take it you don't."

Rich didn't correct her. Nicole turned away. When was the horror going to end? "Thanks for letting me know about the fire inspector's verdict. I haven't found the insurance policy yet, but I'm really tired, so—"

"I need to warn you about something else."

Nicole whirled toward him. He'd stepped so close

she had to crank her head back to look into his eyes. His gaze held sorrow and sympathy. She held herself rigid to keep from yielding to his warmth and stepping into arms that would hold her tight if she issued the invitation.

"Some loudmouth folks around town are jumping to conclusions about your grandparents and the Elling kidnapping."

Nicole stared off in the direction of the cookie jar in the shape of a goose on Grandma Jan's counter. "We sort of expected that, didn't we?"

"Yeah, but I didn't want you to be blindsided when you go out into the community."

"Well, thanks, then." She backed away from Rich. "Have a good evening." The trite expression flowed out her mouth even as she wished him to stay, or for herself to go somewhere far, far from death and fire and a good-looking cop that spelled danger to her heart.

"Lock up tight." Rich turned and grasped the doorknob. "The night-duty officer will do frequent drive-bys, but don't hesitate to call at the least hint of something out of the ordinary."

"Will do."

Then he was gone, and Nicole sought solace in a book. When she couldn't remember what she read, she tried a sitcom, but didn't crack a smile because all the funny lines fell on deaf ears. At last the news came on. There was a segment on the incidents in

Ellington. A brief statement from Stan, the fire inspector, revealed last night's fire as arson, but there was no comment from the Chief of Police. The next shot showed a scowling crowd of townsfolk standing on a downtown sidewalk around a microphone extended by a woman reporter.

"Them Kellers been part of this community all my life," said a craggy-faced man dressed like a farmer or laborer. "Before I was born, I guess. Always did think they was too good to be true. Upstanding bank president?" The man snorted. "Kidnapping babykiller is more like it."

People around him nodded. Nicole clapped a hand over her mouth and swallowed bile.

The reporter put the microphone to her own lips. "It hasn't been confirmed that the bones found on the Keller property belong to the kidnapped Samuel Elling."

The self-appointed community spokesperson sneered. "What other baby's gone missing around here?"

Vocal agreement chorused through the group.

"What's going on?" A woman's voice blared in the background and heads turned.

The familiar figure of Darlene Hooper stepped out of her beauty shop behind the group. The beautician had given Nicole's hair a trim more than once when Nicole was a little girl. Now the woman had aged to the point that she used a cane, and she stabbed it toward the crowd.

"You ought to be ashamed of yourselves, talking about fine folks before the evidence is in. You're all cruising for a lawsuit when the Kellers come out innocent."

Heads lowered and people shuffled away, all except the blabbermouth, who turned toward the microphone, hunting another two seconds of fame. The reporter darted past him, microphone extended toward Darlene.

"What do you know about the recent incidents in Ellington?"

Darlene glared toward the camera. "I know what kind of folks the Kellers have always been. More good-hearted people you couldn't hope to find. Whoever hurt that baby, it wasn't them. And if I ever hear who hurt Jan, I wouldn't mind schooling them at the end of my cane." She turned and disappeared into her shop.

The reporter faced the camera, gaze alight. "As you can see, emotion runs high in the citizens of the little town of Ellington over the discovery of the remains of the Rose Garden Baby and subsequent events, including a violent attack on the woman whose backyard served as a burial ground and the fire that destroyed her downtown shop."

The reporter babbled on, advising viewers to tune in to future newscasts for breaking developments.

Nicole jammed her thumb on the remote button, and the television went dead. Too bad she couldn't turn off the echoes of those cruel voices in her head so easily. Thank goodness for decent people like Darlene Hooper.

The phone rang, but inertia held Nicole on the couch. She didn't want to talk to anyone right now. But what if it was the hospital with news about her grandmother? Nicole sprang up and scurried to the phone on the entry table.

"Hello?" Her greeting came out rather breathy.

"I didn't wake you up, did I? You sound like you've been exercising." It was Rich.

"No, that's all right. I thought maybe it was the hospital calling about Grandma."

"Just me. I—um… Well, I was just wondering if you watched—"

"Yes, I saw the news broadcast."

Rich let out a sound akin to a growl. "I wasn't sure whether to call or not. If you hadn't seen it, I didn't want to bring unnecessary hurt. But then I figured you'd probably watch the news, if not now, then tomorrow sometime. They're likely to reair that segment. Juicy, you know. Anyway—" he huffed a long breath "—I just wanted to tell you not to pay any attention to Ralph Reinert. He hangs with the wild crowd around Mason Elling."

"Ralph's a bit old for that bunch, isn't he?"

"No one else will put up with his sophomoric

behavior. To put it bluntly, he's known around town as a loudmouth. His opinion doesn't count for much."

Nicole traced her finger through dust on the entry table. She'd let her grandmother down already, not keeping the place up. The inane thought passed through her brain then she swatted it away. "I could tell this Ralph guy was a lot more talk than intelligence, but there are obviously folks who agree with him."

"Every gasbag has his following."

A tiny titter left Nicole's mouth. "Thanks. You did manage to cheer me up. Some anyway."

Her heart wouldn't be in her laugh until he told her he'd caught the perp who killed a baby, and that it was neither of her grandparents.

Rich hunkered down in his police unit, gaze scanning the display area and parking lot of the second implement company in town. The dealership sat on the north edge of the city next to open fields. For camouflage, Rich had parked in the far end of the lot near some used machinery. Between him and the customer parking area lay a wide strip of grass that could use the services of one of the mowers he was guarding.

A yawn overtook him, and he shook sleep fumes from his head then sucked a mouthful from his coffee mug. The bitter, lukewarm brew hit his throat like sludge, but he forced it down. No way was he going to conk out on this impromptu, one-man stakeout. If the equipment thieves went after one implement dealership, they could well go after the other. But would it be tonight? Sometimes cop work was simply playing a hunch.

Rich had taken the task on by himself and on the sly because his police force was getting spread mighty thin between extra drive-bys at the Keller home, increased patrols downtown following the fire and the continued burglaries. He was pulling a double shift, but catching the larcenous outfit would be well worth the loss of a little shut-eye. Besides, tomorrow—well, today, actually, was his day off, and he could grab extra z's.

So far, the area around the dealership remained peaceful. Tractors and combines sat illuminated by three tall yard lights. The smaller equipment, like lawn mowers and garden tillers, hunkered in the shadows next to the building.

Rich checked his watch—4:00 a.m. If nothing happened soon, he'd hang it up for the night. The sun wouldn't peek over the horizon for another couple of hours, but the night sky was already graying. A predawn breeze wafted through the partially open driver's-side window, carrying a whiff of ripe alfalfa from a nearby field and a faint noise that hadn't been there before.

Was it the sound of tires creeping across gravel?

Rich stiffened, gaze sifting through the darkness

for something out of place. Sure enough. The outline of a pick-up and trailer took shape on the approach from the county road near the side of the building. There was no reason for the owner or an employee to enter the area from that direction, and certainly not at this hour. Rich held himself still, watching, cautioning himself to patience. The perps needed to make a move on the equipment before he nabbed them.

Two dark-clad figures, shadows in the dimness, approached a riding lawn mower. A sharp snap announced the chain anchoring the mower's wheels had been sliced with a bolt cutter. The pair began guiding the mower to the rear of the trailer.

Gotcha!

Rich picked up his radio and quietly told the dispatcher to send backup. Then he flipped on his lights and bleeped his siren. The perps went rigid. The saying "deer in the headlights" could have been written just for them. Ski masks and Western-style duster coats cloaked their identities, but Rich would know soon enough.

He climbed out of his unit and stood behind his door, gun drawn. "Hands in the air. Don't move a muscle."

The perps complied with the hand raising, but their heads swiveled away from him. Movement near the pickup caught his eye. A flame flickered and caught, as if someone had lit a giant candle. Then the flame sailed through the air. Glass shattered on impact with a nearby piece of equipment, and fire exploded. Rich dived into his vehicle. The cuts on his back from the incident at the shop pulled and stung. A wave of sharp heat chased him then ebbed to steady warmth. Being flash-broiled was getting old.

Rich sat up. The night bloomed with fire in the grass in front of his vehicle. Doors slammed and tires squealed as the thieves roared away. Rich peeled out backward away from the fire, then skirted the blaze, and shot toward the county road, but the pickup and trailer had disappeared.

Derek, who was on night duty, arrived to back him up a few minutes too late, and then the volunteer fire department turned out to douse the grass fire. The sky had lightened to pewter, and the turf still smoldered by the time Terry pulled up. He climbed out of his black-and-white, eyes bleary and bloodshot. Rich gave him a sharp look.

"Short night, early call-out," the man clipped in response.

Tell me about it. Rich kept the thought to himself. "Apparently, our equipment thieves know how to make Molotov cocktails."

"You gotta be kidding me."

"This look like a joke?" Rich jerked a thumb toward the smoking grass.

"So these guys bombed the sewing shop, too."

"Looks like it."

"Should give us more evidence to piece together if it's the same perps."

"You'd think, but unless they got careless this time, and there are fingerprints or some other evidence on the glass shards, we're pretty much still at square one. I didn't even get a make or model on the vehicle, though the trailer was a flatbed with low sides."

Terry snorted. "About a dime a dozen around here."

"You got it." Rich pointed toward the gravel approach the thieves had used. "You're our best tire specialist. See what you can do about finding a clear set of tread marks. Maybe they'll match what we found at the other implement dealership."

"Will do, Chief." Terry strode past his boss.

A heavy dousing of Old Spice tweaked Rich's nostrils. Terry obviously hadn't had time to shower due to the emergency call-out. Which woman's cologne was his deputy trying to cover up this time?

Rich went over to Derek. "Look into the whereabouts of Ralph Reinert the evening of the fire at the shop and also this morning. He's been way too vocal about the Kellers to suit me, and he's just the sort of knothead who'd think of lifting small equipment as a sideline career."

"I'm on it." The young cop jerked a nod.

"And I'm heading for the sack. We won't be locking up any thieves today."

"Well, maybe you scared them enough they'll lay off for a while."

"I hope not. They need to keep at it so we can catch them."

Derek pursed his lips. "Funny the local grapevine hasn't caught wind of anyone bragging or letting a careless word slip. It's hard to keep anything under wraps in a small town like this."

"Keep the feelers out there." Rich walked away, frowning.

The kid had a point. Usually, it wasn't much of a challenge to get information on penny-ante drug dealers or shoplifters, but no one seemed to know a thing about these thefts. And the identity of the thieves wasn't the only secret well guarded around here. Something terrible had happened in the Elling mansion years ago. He'd stake his badge on it. And the kidnapping was the tip of the iceberg.

What had Goody Hanson meant about "those poor women"? Nicole interpreted the statement to mean the hardships of the Elling wives over the decades. Rich had checked her research, and she was spot on. Henry the Eighth didn't have much on the Elling men. But the context of Goody's outburst smacked of a specific reference to when Derek's grandmother worked for the Ellings. What did the old woman know, and why couldn't she speak of it without tipping off her rocker?

Rich shuddered. A part of him didn't want to probe the darkness and find the answer. But even an ugly truth was better than a beautiful lie that protected the guilty and wounded innocents like Nicole. Even if the facts proved one or both of her grandparents guilty in that infant's death, wouldn't the knowledge be easier to bear than forever wondering?

ELEVEN

After a short night's sleep, disturbed by every creak and groan of the old house, Nicole was unable to stay in bed past the first birdsong. She found the insurance policy on the shop shortly after sunup in a stack of papers removed during the police search from a drawer in her grandmother's china hutch. She read the name of the agency and smacked her forehead. Of course, Grandma would take her coverage through the bank where Grandpa Frank worked his way up from teller to president.

Nicole flopped onto the couch, wiped out before the day hardly began. Now that she knew who to contact about the insurance, she needed the official word to go ahead and have the debris cleared up. She pulled out her cell and punched in Rich's number. The connection started to ring and she gasped. What was she thinking? It wasn't even 6:30 a.m. Rich must be sleeping. She started to close her phone but his crisp voice answered on the first ring.

"Oh, I'm sorry, Rich," she burst out. "I shouldn't

have called so early. Did I wake you up? You certainly sound chipper."

He let out a dry chuckle. "Chipper? No. Awake? Yes. I haven't been to bed yet. I just got home from a crime scene."

Nicole groaned. "Another robbery?"

"Attempted. They got away when one of them chucked a Molotov cocktail at me."

"Are you hurt?" Nicole's throat tightened.

"Not a scratch or a singe. More than I can say for the other evening outside your grandmother's shop."

"Does this mean that these thieves are responsible for what happened there?"

"It's a pretty strong connection."

"Maybe they stole sewing machines and then burned the place to hide the crime." Several beats of silence answered her. "You don't think theft was involved?"

"I can't rule it out, but stealing household appliances hasn't been among their interests. But to eliminate the possibility, have the crew you hire for cleanup check to see if the remains of sewing machines are among the debris."

Nicole ran her fingers through a rat's nest of bed hair that she hadn't combed out yet this morning. "Cleanup is what I was calling about. Do I have your permission to get it done?"

"The sooner the better. That kind of wreckage is a hazard to the public."

"I'll get something going as soon as possible then."

"Have you called a security company about wiring the house for intruders?"

"Done," she assured him, "but they're not sure how soon they'll get here."

"I'll call and jack them up a bit. See if it'll get faster action for you."

"Thanks. I appreciate it."

They ended the call. The concern in Rich's voice touched Nicole's heart. Then again, maybe she should set no store by it. He might be mostly thinking about his staff that could ease up on the extra drive-bys after the house had a security system. It would be best to interpret the note of caring in his tone as impersonal. After all, she and Rich could never be anything more than friends. For the sake of her own sanity she should probably keep her distance from him. Hard to do when this case kept throwing them together.

Gusting a long breath, Nicole stretched out on the couch. She could afford to relax for a few minutes. It was too early to call anyone about insurance or cleanup anyway.

She stirred awake to the neighbor's dog barking. How long had she slept? Nicole lifted her head and looked at the wall clock. Yikes! She'd been totally zonked for more than three hours. It was after nine. She sat up and stretched. But the z's had sure felt good.

A quick call to the hospital yielded the usual report. Jan Keller was stable, but still comatose. Next, Nicole called the insurance agency at the bank. The agent was warm and sympathetic. He even recommended an excavation crew. But after a ten-minute conversation, she closed the connection with her stomach dropped somewhere near her toes. Grandma had insured the shop, all right, but at a rate that might have replaced the business twenty-five years ago. The payout would nowhere near cover reopening the business at today's costs.

"I'm so sorry," the agent had said. "I kept recommending that Jan increase her coverage, but she didn't want to pay a higher premium."

Nicole had assured the man that she didn't hold him responsible for her grandmother's decisions. She didn't add that she understood his frustration with her stubborn, frugal grandmother. Now the store might never be rebuilt. Grandma would be devastated. And that wasn't all. *She* was devastated. Nicole hadn't realized quite how deeply she was emotionally invested in her idea for a machine embroidery business. There had to be a way!

Nicole sat down at the kitchen table with a piece of paper and her checkbook calculator. Twenty minutes of noodling and doodling later, she sat back with a smile. The dream might still come true. She'd have to deplete her husband's pension and the life insurance benefits she'd socked away, but she'd end up owning a large share of the business outright. Grandma could still have her yard goods and sewing notions, and maybe…hopefully—*oh, please, God!*—they could both be happy in a symbiotic setup.

There was a lot to do between then and now. Nicole picked up her cell phone and called the number the insurance agent had given her for the excavation company. They agreed to start at the shop tomorrow. Now she could use the rest of the day to work on setting the house to rights. Her stomach let out a yowl. First things first. A little sustenance. She went to the refrigerator. Pretty slim pickings. She took out the milk, sniffed it, and made a face. Sour. A trip to the grocery store was in order.

Nicole gathered up her purse and headed out to her car by the garage. She opened the driver's-side door and a stench assaulted her. She backed away with her hand over her mouth and nose. Had a skunk invaded her vehicle? No, the smell was different. Nothing appeared wrong in the front seat. She peered through the window into the back. A garbage bag sat on the floor between the passenger seat and the rear of the driver's seat.

How did that get in there? Hadn't she locked her car door when she returned from the Elling home the night the garbage bag went missing? She searched her memory and came up blank. She'd been upset about finding those bones and the weirdness at the Elling place. Maybe she didn't lock up, and whoever moved the garbage bag between the time Grandma put it out and Nicole came looking had stuffed it in her car. Then the next day when she drove to the shop and back with the police, the bag hadn't been in there long enough to ferment whatever was inside. Nor had she looked into the back that morning. She hadn't driven the car since.

Who had moved the garbage bag? And why?

Her grandmother seemed to have believed the garbage bag had been collected by the city truck. Obviously, someone else hadn't wanted that to happen. Or was this just a prank? It would be less threatening to believe the bag got into her car as a product of idle meanness, but she couldn't convince herself the incident was so simple. The bag had been placed in her car on purpose, and she was meant to find it. Her breaths came shallow and rapid. She should report this find to the police—to Rich—and let them handle the potential evidence. But she couldn't. Not yet. She had to know what was inside before they did.

Nicole hustled into the house and returned with the garage key. Inside the garage, she donned a pair of gardening gloves then retrieved the garbage bag from her car, leaving the door open to air out the vehicle. She spread old newspapers over a bare spot on the cement floor. Poised to dump the contents of the bag onto the newspapers, she hesitated, heartsick.

Did this sack of refuse contain evidence that stunk worse than the rotten garbage?

Rich came wide awake around the 1:00 p.m. hour. How did the regular night-shift guys do it? Sleeping during the day was a hopeless proposition for him. He got up, shaved and showered, and called the office for an update on open cases, even though it was his day off.

Terry was in and reported on results from the MBCA office on fingerprints, though nothing had come in on DNA yet. That sort of thing took a lot longer than the TV shows made it look like. Prints on the bat came back primarily to Jan Keller. A few degraded ones were from her son, Nicole's father, and some other old ones came from an unknown donor. Rich speculated out loud that they were from Frank, Nicole's grandfather, and Terry grunted agreement. No other fresh prints were found, and the bat showed no signs of having been wiped down.

"Which means whoever attacked Jan Keller must have been wearing gloves," Terry concluded.

"What about prints on the bag that contained the infant's remains?" Rich asked.

Paper rustled in the background. "Now, here's where it gets interesting. Two sets of prints on the bag. Judging by size, the smaller are likely from a female or possibly an adolescent."

"No match to Jan?"

"Negative. But the larger set of prints, likely male, are a match to the unidentified prints on the bat."

"Frank Keller." Dread clutched Rich's chest.

"Strong probability. Sorry, Chief. I know you were hoping none of the Kellers were involved."

The guy sounded genuinely sympathetic, which was a surprise. But then, he seemed to have his eye on Nicole, too, and wouldn't want to get on her bad side, either. Rich suppressed a rush of jealous protectiveness.

"We still have no one to question, much less arrest," he clipped out.

Until and unless Jan woke up. He didn't verbalize that thought. Even though there was no physical evidence connecting Jan to the buried infant, her behavior following the discovery suggested she knew something. Provided she retained her mental faculties, would she be more or less apt to come clean after the attack in the attic?

"Anything else on the fire or this morning's incident?" Rich went on.

Terry made a game show buzzer sound. "Derek didn't find any prints on the bottle used for the Molotov last night. It was clean, and the same type as the one from the sewing shop."

"Sun Drop?" The brand of soft drink was

manufactured by a local bottling company and regionally distributed, mostly in cans, but some folks paid extra for the nostalgic bottles. "That narrows our suspects to anyone in west central Minnesota."

"Maybe not. I hunted pretty hard for Ralph Reinert this morning, and he seems to have skipped the area. He didn't show up for work this morning, and his car is gone. None of his usual cronies knows where he is."

"He's definitely a person of interest. Did you put out an APB on his vehicle?"

Terry snorted. "I didn't enroll in the police academy last week."

Rich chuckled. "I had to ask."

"Right."

"In your canvas of Reinert's known associates, did you talk to Mason Elling?"

"Nope. The Elling kid seems to be laying low, too, not haunting his usual watering holes."

"Maybe he's got a reason to stay home and out of sight."

"I could pay a visit to the mansion on the hill."

"Leave it. You've got enough on your plate. I'll track the kid down tomorrow when I'm back on duty." While he was at it, he'd see if he could finally corner Fern for an interview. The woman hadn't called him back since his last attempt to see her. Not that he was surprised.

Rich ended the call to the office and then wandered

around his lonely house. There were household projects he could tackle, but he didn't have the heart for them. His whole being was occupied with this tangled mess of cases that seemed to somehow be connected...and the tether led straight to the Kellers.

Nicole, the innocent party, had been stuck with enormous issues, not to mention a massive household cleanup project. That part was his fault. Rich checked his watch—2:00 p.m. Maybe she'd welcome a helping hand at straightening up the place. The Keller residence was a focal point of this cold case gone sizzling. It couldn't hurt to spend more time there. He picked up his phone and punched in her cell number. That way, if she was out and about, he'd still catch her.

The phone rang and rang. Just when he thought the call would go to voice mail, she answered.

"H-Hello? Rich? Is that you?"

"Your caller ID is correct. Did I interrupt a well-deserved nap?" She sounded groggy. *No, more like dazed and upset.*

Nicole spluttered a laugh. "No, I wasn't sleeping. Not with all I've got to do around here. I'm just... overwhelmed. Distracted. Whatever you want to call it."

"How about I give you a hand? I've got the day off, and I'm bouncing around my empty house like a pinball."

"I don't know, Rich. You don't have to feel like you should—"

"Are you telling me you couldn't use another pair of willing hands?"

The connection went silent long enough for him to wonder if she'd closed the call.

"Okay. I guess I could use the help."

"I'll be right there."

Whistling, Rich grabbed his keys and his wallet and climbed into his off-duty vehicle—a sports-model Ranger pickup. Nicole had sounded jittery, but she had plenty of reason to feel that way. And good cause to wonder if she should let him in that house, but he was glad she said yes. Too glad. His poor heart was running big risks, and a reckless part of him didn't care one bit.

An unsmiling Nicole opened the front door to him. He followed her through the foyer into the living room. Most of the furniture remained out of place.

"I'll put your muscle to work with that to start with." She motioned toward the couch that stood kitty-corner in the middle of the room.

Rich moved toward the piece of furniture. Nicole darted ahead of him and grabbed the far end. Together they put the couch back in its place then worked steadily to set the rest of the room to rights. She must really be skittish of him because she didn't talk except to give directions and kept her distance.

"I'm done in Grandma's bedroom and mine," she said, "but not much else. How about you take the dining room, and I'll tackle the kitchen."

"Sounds like a plan." What else could he do but let her be the boss?

Over the next few hours, they worked through the house, room by room. Nicole always made sure they weren't in the same room. Accidentally or on purpose? Rich battled disappointment that she seemed determined to hold herself aloof. But wasn't that a good thing? Hadn't he determined a similar course of action where the attractive Nicole Mattson was concerned? Why couldn't he convince his heart to chalk her up as a missed opportunity?

They finished the last rooms on the second floor and then met in the hallway. Nicole eyed the open doorway to the attic as if a monster might emerge from the stairwell at any time.

"We might as well get this over with." She marched toward the attic.

Rich hurried after her. So that's what had been bugging her. Of course! She'd have to face the spot her grandmother had lain bleeding. The stain would still be on the floorboards.

"Just a minute," he called.

Oblivious, Nicole charged ahead and started up the stairs just as Rich reached the bottom. On the third step, she let out a sound like a half sigh, half sob and went limp. Her body collapsed backward.

Exclaiming, Rich lifted his arms and caught her. The impact of her slight frame drove him a step backward.

Cradling her limp form, he lowered her to the floor. Nicole was out cold. Did she faint? Was she ill? Her skin was bleached white, not hot or flushed with fever. A rank smell wafted from her hair. Rich sniffed the sleeve of her shirt. Clean. But her skin smelled faintly of the same decay as her hair, like a Dumpster diver who'd had time to change clothes but not enough time to take a shower.

Was this telltale odor the real reason Nicole had put space between them? What had she been doing? Going through neighborhood garbage bins looking for that missing bag? Or maybe she found it and what she'd discovered inside had scared her silly. Rich's pulse stalled. Would she really keep something like that from him? With a sick feeling, he knew the answer. Anyone in her situation might decide to protect the living over seeking justice for the dead.

What should he do with his suspicion? Confront her? No, that move would be counterproductive—not only to his case, but to their relationship. Maybe if he gave her some space to process whatever had so shocked her, she would come to him of her own free will. He'd wait. Not indefinitely, but for a little while.

Right now, he needed to see if he could wake Nicole from her faint. He patted her pale cheek.

"Wake up, honey." The endearment slipped from his lips, and he didn't want to call it back.

A slight groan met his efforts. Her eyelids fluttered and then popped open. "Wh-what happened?"

"I think you passed out."

"Me? Pass out? I've never done such a thing in my life." Nicole sat up under her own power, and a noise rumbled from her stomach. She put a hand to her middle.

"When was the last time you had something to eat?"

Nicole's forehead puckered. "Um, I ate a tuna fish sandwich yesterday evening. I was going to go to the grocery store this morning, but—" Her gaze fell away from his. "Well, you know how crazy things have been."

With an effort, Rich kept himself from erupting with a barrage of questions. She must have run into a big distraction—like the missing garbage bag. Then he called and insisted on coming over, and the rest was history.

Rich helped Nicole to her feet. "We're going downstairs and order a pizza. Then you're going to relax with your feet up and a cool beverage while I clean up that bad spot in the attic."

"Oh, would you?"

He'd walk across the Sahara in a snowsuit to

receive the adoration of those big brown eyes. If his chest expanded any more, he'd need a bigger shirt. He'd just better remember that if she was hiding something from him, they would be working on opposite sides of the law.

TWELVE

After they consumed the pizza and Rich left, Nicole meandered from room to room in the big old house. Now that the mess was tidied up, she was left with nothing on her plate but to stew over what she'd discovered in that garbage bag. And the fact that she hadn't turned her find over to Rich.

That guy was amazing! So kind and thoughtful, funny and gentle. But a good cop, tough when he needed to be.

What was the matter with her? She couldn't keep the information—sketchy as it was—away from the law. But she needed time to think about the cryptic remains of a torn letter she'd pieced together from the debris. Most of the flowery script had been soaked completely away in the meat grease contained in the garbage bag. What remained decipherable contained no "To" or "From" information. Maybe "sweet baby S" on one scrap wasn't even talking about Samuel Elling. Maybe the letter had nothing to do with the kidnapping. Maybe the bones she'd found belonged to some other child.

Nicole plopped down at the kitchen table and rubbed her forehead with the tips of her fingers. Why bother playing these games of denial with herself? Of course the letter she found was connected to the remains under the rose garden. Why else would her grandmother be so bent on destroying it, and who else would "baby S" be than Samuel Elling? But accepting those deductions raised a crop of new questions.

Who sent the letter? A woman, judging by the handwriting, but there were no addresses on the ripped-up remains of the envelope—which meant it hadn't passed through the mail—just the words *Urgent! Please read right away!* in the same ornate script as the letter. At least, Nicole could rule out her grandmother as the author. Grandma Jan's handwriting was a sturdy block print. But was she the recipient of the letter? If not, then how did she get it and from whom? Grandpa Frank? If so, did he give it to his wife or did she find the haunting missive among his effects after his death? Nicole couldn't imagine her steady, rather stodgy, grandfather receiving a clandestine note from another woman.

A disbelieving laugh started in Nicole's throat then lodged there and became a lump. Impossible to imagine Grandpa burying an infant under his roses, but someone had. And Rich had noted that it was likely someone who cared about the child. Grandpa Frank loved children. She slammed fisted hands onto the table then pressed them against her eyes.

This whole situation was too much to handle by herself. If only she could unload on Rich. He'd understand. He'd say the right thing. He always did. But then he'd have to, to be a cop.

She lifted her head. Hadn't she noticed that smug investigator look on his face when he returned from the attic? Nicole went rigid. Did he snoop in her room and find the letter? She charged up the stairs two at a time and strong-armed her mattress several inches up from the box spring. Breath gusted between her teeth. The greasy, taped together scraps remained in the plastic bag right where she'd left it.

Nicole let the mattress drop back into place. But that didn't mean he hadn't found the letter and read it. She sank onto the edge of the bed. No, if Rich had found this evidence, his duty as an officer would have compelled him to confiscate it.

Then why had he looked like a bloodhound on a scent when he came downstairs? She knew that look from her dad and her husband. Rich had found a new lead. In the attic? But what?

Nicole trotted up the steps and gazed around. Not only had Rich scrubbed away the stain on the floor-boards, but he'd righted stacks of boxes and set the clutter into neat rows. The contents of the attic still needed a good sorting and weeding, but at least there were aisles to walk through the area. Her grandfather's school memorabilia had also been put away in his old trunk. Grandma had taken Nicole through all those items shortly after Grandpa died—a painful, precious celebration of a life well lived. Could there possibly have been something in there that pointed suspicion at Frank Keller?

Kneeling by the trunk, she opened the lid. A letter jacket lay folded neatly on top of the contents. Nicole removed it and began digging through the keepsakes. Grandpa's parents had documented his life extensively. Some school papers from kindergarten were in here, yellowed and brittle. A set of three volumes caught her eye—Grandpa's yearbooks. She dug them out. In the first one she looked at, Frank Keller's picture was under the sophomore class. In the next one, she found him under the freshman class. The third volume was from his junior year.

Nicole rocked back on her heels. Where was Grandpa's senior yearbook? There's no way he collected one from every year of his high school life and neglected the most significant year of all. Did Rich take the book? Nicole shook her head. No, he'd come down the stairs with nothing in his hands but the cleaning bucket and supplies. He couldn't have hidden a find any bigger than something he could tuck in his pocket.

Or maybe Rich had noticed the same thing she did—the senior yearbook was missing. That meant someone had taken it. Someone like the person who attacked her grandmother only a few feet from this trunk.

Prickles swarmed across Nicole's skin. That book must contain information the attacker didn't want known. Rich would have come to the same conclusion, and he'd be on the trail of a copy first thing tomorrow. Nicole needed to beat him to it. Whatever was hidden in that book, she wanted to know it first, if only to steel herself for whatever was to come regarding her grandparents' involvement in that long-ago kidnapping. Maybe then she could make herself turn that letter over to Rich.

The next morning, Nicole met the excavation crew downtown at the remains of the shop. Holding reopening plans in the forefront of her mind, the heavy sense of loss began to give place to anticipation. Now, if only she could convince her grandmother to feel the same way. *Please, God, let me have the opportunity to present the new business plan to an awake and aware woman.* Even if they clashed over the idea, that alternative was far better than dealing with the possibility of brain damage or even death.

Nicole instructed the excavators to keep a log of major items, such as sewing machines, they discovered in the debris. The crew chief acknowledged her request and said that Police Chief Rich Hendricks had already instructed them to run a tally in order to determine whether theft was connected to the arson.

Rich was ahead of her again. Was he also ahead of her in finding a copy of that yearbook?

Nicole turned away from the burned-out shop, hands in her jeans pockets. A smattering of gawkers had gathered on the sidewalk across the street as the crew began their task. The cleanup activity was as good as a circus in this small community. Gazes avoided hers, and no one approached to ask about Jan Keller. Was someone in that group angry enough to have set the fire? They all looked sufficiently uncomfortable to have been responsible. Or maybe that was because Jan Keller's granddaughter was studying them, and they had no clue what to say.

Sorrow dug an aching pit in Nicole's heart. Look what damage suspicion had already done to her family. The only way to fix this was to find out what really happened half a century ago. Despite the doubts that clamored against her faith, she had to believe the truth would exonerate her grandparents.

Darlene's Beauty Shop caught her eye. Hadn't the yearbooks shown Darlene to be a classmate of Grandpa Frank's? Maybe the beautician would have a copy of their senior yearbook.

Energized, Nicole made a beeline for the store, ignoring the regular crosswalk. If the police actually ticketed people for jaywalking around here, everybody in town would owe a mint. She found Darlene holding court on a stool behind the sales counter, while the two beauticians who worked for her tended to clients. According to Nicole's grandmother, Darlene welcomed her midseventies with the energy of a fifty-year-old and no inclination to retire, but her legs would no longer tolerate standing for long hours. The shop owner stayed busy collecting fees, selling hair-care products and gabbing with the clients awaiting their turns in the chairs.

The gabbing went silent as Nicole crossed the waiting area to the counter. Darlene greeted her with a big grin that faded to brow-puckered concern.

"How is that tough old bird grandmother of yours doing?" the woman asked in her Mae West voice.

Nicole flickered a smile. "She is a tough one. I'll give her that. The doctor said she's lucky she has such a hard head."

Darlene laughed and a few snickers chimed in from the patrons.

"Grandma's hanging in there." Nicole hauled in a deep breath of beauty shop air scented with perm solution and hair spray. "I've got a favor to ask of you. Could we talk in private?"

"Anything!" Darlene climbed down from her stool and picked up her cane. "Kay, you're in charge for a little while," she said to one of the beauticians.

"We're retiring to my mansion." She followed the words with a throaty chuckle.

Nicole trailed her hostess through a door at the rear of the shop and found herself in a tiny, well-lived-in apartment. The place probably hadn't been redecorated in decades, but the clutter was more cozy than messy.

Darlene turned, planted both hands on the top of her cane, and fixed Nicole with eagle eyes. "What can I do to help?"

"I'm looking for a copy of my grandfather's senior yearbook. You were classmates."

The beautician's painted-on brows arched upward. "Never expected that one. I won't ask why, though I assume it has something to do with what happened to that poor little infant." She caned her way over to a metal bookshelf. "For the record, I don't for a second believe Frank or Jan had a thing to do with kidnapping or hurting a child."

"Thanks," Nicole said. "Neither do I."

"Good girl. Hang in there. This town'll come to its senses eventually. They're good eggs, mostly, just confused. Ah, here it is." Darlene pulled a slim volume from one of the shelves. "I'm a sentimental old hoss. I actually leaf through these from time to time. Good for a laugh." She shrugged and handed the book to Nicole. "If it's anything you can check out right here, I'd prefer not to let the book off the premises."

"I'm not even sure what I'm looking for, but I can browse here as well as anywhere."

"Have a seat." Darlene motioned toward a bulky couch sporting a plaid cover over the original upholstery. "Take your time. You know where I'll be." The beautician fluttered her fingers and headed out front.

As soon as the door closed behind her hostess, Nicole settled onto the couch, clutching her prize in both hands. Her heart thudded erratically against her ribs. What secret would she find within these pages that was worth nearly killing an old woman to protect?

Within a half hour, Nicole had her answer. She'd gotten so caught up in reading the sometimes funny, sometimes poignant autographs scrawled on the pages by classmates—including a brief quip by her grandfather—that she almost missed the photo embedded in a collage from that year's prom.

No surprise that her grandfather wasn't posing proudly beside her grandmother under a floral archway. Grandma Jan wasn't from Ellington. Nicole's grandparents had met while Frank was attending college to become an accountant. But maybe Nicole had uncovered why Grandma couldn't stand Hannah Breyer.

Frank and Hannah had been high school sweethearts.

Had Grandpa and his old flame picked up where

they left off when he and his bride returned to Ellington? She could see how Hannah might do anything, including seduce a married man, to try to get out of that awful Elling house. Was the baby under the rose garden Grandpa's and Hannah's? That would mean the child wasn't Samuel Elling like everyone assumed.

Nicole's pulse fluttered. She struggled between hope and horror. How awful for Grandma if Grandpa strayed. Shame on him! But at least if the child wasn't the Elling baby, the stigma of kidnap and murder would lift.

Maybe Hannah went away somewhere to give birth and then returned to Ellington with her little surprise for Frank. A scrap of the letter Nicole found in the trash had said "after all we've been to each other." Had the missive been a demand that Frank meet his lover and child somewhere? Then what happened? Something accidental, of course. No way Grandpa Frank would hurt a baby. But if he would betray his wife and bury his love child in secret, why would he draw the line at—

What was she thinking! Nicole slammed the yearbook shut. This whole speculative scenario stunk. None of it rang true, because it didn't depict the man Nicole had known all her life. Maybe the photo of Hannah and Frank together didn't mean anything. Lots of high schoolers went to prom together on a casual basis. Then why was this issue of the year-book stolen from the Keller attic?

Nicole flipped Darlene's book open again and scanned pages scrawled with personal autographs. Maybe the clue wasn't the prom photo. Maybe it was something a classmate had written in Grandpa's book. In that case, whatever had been said might be lost forever into the hands of whoever didn't want their sins uncovered.

There was one person who might know how much stock Nicole should put in the prom photo. Hannah Breyer. But a chat with her meant another trip to the house on the hill. Nicole's stomach turned. But then, she'd swim across a river infested with alligators to finally lay all these terrors and suspicions to rest.

Rich got off the phone with the accountant who was going over the sewing shop's books. She wasn't done with the project by any means, but so far had found no irregularities to report. In fact, she commended whoever had kept the financial records. They were impeccable. Good for Jan Keller, but a dead end for his investigation. Not that Rich had held high hopes this avenue of inquiry would hit pay dirt. But maybe it would yet. He'd give the accountant more time. And then there was this other thing….

He picked up the old school yearbook laying on the corner of his desk. He'd found the volume in the town library as soon as it opened this morning. If whoever took the book from Jan Keller's attic had hoped to hide something by swiping it, they'd done a poor job. If anything, the theft had drawn attention to the book, not away from it. Then again, the thief may have hoped the clutter in the attic would mask the missing volume, and no one would go looking for a copy.

Rich opened the book to the prom page and stared at the photo. So Frank Keller and Hannah Breyer had attended prom together. She'd been a very pretty girl back in the day, with an impish, appealing smile. Hannah was a junior and a new kid in town that year. Rich's research showed that Fern was guardian of her teenage sister when she married Simon and moved to Ellington. That didn't allow Frank and Hannah a lot of time to develop a hot romance. Then again, those things could sometimes happen in a flash. Did the relationship continue over the years? If so, what bearing did the liaison have on the baby buried under Frank Keller's rose garden? Those were burning questions. With Frank dead and Jan incapacitated, one person remained with the answers. He could add Hannah to the list of people he needed to talk to in the Elling household.

Rich punched the number into the phone on his desk. Simon answered.

"This is Police Chief Rich Hendricks. I'm coming up there to talk to Fern, Mason and Hannah, and I'm not taking any excuses."

"Excuses?" Simon chuckled. "Just bad timing on your part before. Hannah? What do you want with her?"

"That's between her and me."

"Suit yourself. Come ahead. We're eager to cooperate with the police."

Sure, you are. "I'll be right there."

Within a few minutes, Rich was ushered by a too-smug Simon into a massive living room with a vaulted ceiling. The area was sparsely filled with worn, but high-quality furniture.

Mason slumped on one end of a claw-footed couch, bleary gaze betraying a hangover. Rail-thin Fern perched on the other end of the couch, dressed in a dark-colored skirt and blouse, ankles crossed, hands folded in her lap. Across from Fern, Melody lounged cross-legged in a high-backed easy chair. She was clad in her usual designer elegance, and her hothouse-flower perfume clashed with her mother's rose scent. Melody sported a yellowed bruise high on her right cheekbone that heavy makeup couldn't quite conceal. Had Daddy reached the end of his rope with her expenditures? Knowing Simon, it was a short rope.

Plump Hannah sat, shoulders bowed and head lowered, in the matching chair on the other end of the grouping. From a padded footstool near Hannah's chair Nicole gazed up at him, a becoming flush on her cheeks.

"You beat me here," he said. Her presence wasn't a complete surprise. Her car was parked out front. He might have known she'd pick up on the same clue about the yearbook as he had and decide to talk to the same person—Hannah.

She shrugged and sent him a rueful smile. "Just barely."

Rich looked toward Simon. "Is there someplace I can visit with people individually?"

The man crossed his arms. "We're a family. If the child that was found really is Samuel, we're the victims here. Whatever you have to say and whatever questions you have should be open to all of us."

Nicole bit her lip. She looked as frustrated as he felt. Simon seemed to be maneuvering them both out of the opportunity for private interviews. Rich didn't want what anyone said to be colored by what others in the room might think. Hannah didn't look prepared to utter a sound in this setting. However, he'd learned to play the hand he was dealt. Maybe something would come of this family chat.

"Mason, can you account for your whereabouts the evening Jan's Sewing Room was torched and the early morning of the fire at Ellington Implement?"

The young man scowled and reddened. "Don't try to pin that stuff on me. I'm no firebug. I don't have an alibi if that's what you mean. I was alone and minding my own business both times." His lifted chin dared Rich to prove otherwise.

"Do you know the whereabouts of Ralph Reinert?"

Mason sneered. "That loser? I'm just glad he hasn't been trying to hang out with me and my buddies the past couple of days."

"Answer the question."

"No, I have no idea where Ralph Reinert is. Don't care, either."

That went well. Rich shifted focus. "Hannah? Would you look at me, please?"

No response.

"It's okay." Nicole touched the woman's knee.

Hannah's head slowly lifted. Her gaze was distant, vacant. Not auspicious for getting straight answers.

"How well did you know Frank Keller?" Rich plunged ahead anyway.

"Wh-who?" She blinked at him.

"My grandfather, Frank Keller," Nicole inserted.

Hannah's gaze fell to Nicole, and her posture marginally softened. "You have his eyebrows."

"You knew him well, then?" Nicole's tone edged on husky.

Rich's heart twisted. This must be a highly emotional moment for her.

Hannah stared down at her lap and picked at imaginary lint on her poodle skirt. "He was my friend."

"That's all? Just a friend?" Nicole leaned toward the other woman, knuckles white where her fingers gripped the edges of the footstool.

Hannah's nod was barely perceptible. "And then he left me."

The desperation in her tone, the hint of a wail, set Rich's teeth on edge. There was much more to this story than was going to emerge the way Simon had so deliberately set the scene.

"He left you?" Nicole sank back on her seat. "What do you mean?" Her gaze devoured Hannah, oblivious to anyone else in the room.

"It's okay, Nicole." Rich measured his tone to be soothing but firm.

Her head whipped toward him, and their eyes held for long seconds. Emotions wrestled one another across her face—hope and fear, dread and anticipation. Then her shoulders relaxed, and she inclined her head. *Good girl.* The Elling patriarch wasn't going to get the last laugh. Rich would make sure of that. But for right now, he and Nicole needed to exercise patience. Maybe even caution. Rich had the strangest sense that the family would do anything to keep their dark secrets.

"Isn't anyone going to ask *me* any questions?" A petulant voice entered the conversation.

Rich focused on Simon's wife. The woman's lower lip pouted. Indignation washed her gaze as if she'd been slighted. If Fern had ever been attractive, years of chronic illness had leached away the beauty, leaving a shell of mottled skin and bony angles.

"I'd like you to tell me what you remember about the night your son disappeared," Rich said.

Fern stared somewhere beyond Rich's shoulder. "Sammy woke up crying in the night. That wasn't unusual for him, and he was teething. I went to him and soothed him and put him back in his crib. Then the next morning, when he didn't wake up at his usual time, I went in to check on him, and he was gone."

The words came out in a near monotone, as if she was reciting a lesson learned by rote. In fact, what she said was almost verbatim the quote contained in the old police report.

Rich frowned. "You don't remember anyone showing unusual attention to your son around the time of the kidnapping...someone you met around town, someone who came in to visit, a repair person?"

"Everyone was always fawning over Sammy. He was a beautiful baby." A wild-eyed glare accompanied Fern's statement, as if she was indignant about the question.

Or maybe she was jealous about all the attention shown her child. Could any mother resent her offspring for stealing the limelight? This household was so twisted, anything was possible. He was also getting nowhere fast, except for some very bad vibes.

"If you think of anything else, be sure to call me," he told Fern. Like that would happen, but he too could spout stock statements. "Nicole, shall we be going?"

"But—"

"I'll walk you out to your car."

She gave him a disgusted look, but stood up. She'd had some success getting Hannah to cooperate a few days ago, but Simon wasn't about to allow a repeat. Besides, his gut said he should get Nicole out of this house. Now.

"Do not darken our doorway again, Mrs. Mattson." Simon's tone could have frozen a penguin. "Members of your family are not welcome in this house anymore."

Nicole's eyes widened. "Surely, you don't think my grandparents had anything to do with—"

"The more I think about the situation, the more I *do* think exactly that. Any reasonable person would come to that conclusion, and I pray that Frank and Jan will rot in—"

"That'll be enough!" Rich took a step toward the Elling patriarch.

The man glared at him, face a mottled purple. Quite likely no one, with the possible exception of his father, Seth, had ever told Simon to hold his tongue. Their gazes held, and Rich fully intended to take whatever action necessary to stop this man from inflicting one more ounce of pain on Nicole. Simon must have read Rich's resolve, because his chin lowered, and he clamped his lips shut.

Nicole scurried from the room, shoulders hunched and tears in her eyes. Rich sent Simon one more warning look and stalked out behind her. She charged ahead through the front door, but he caught up with her as she started to open her car door and placed a hand on her shoulder.

She didn't turn and look at him. "Thank you for that small mercy."

"Anytime. Let me know if anyone at all bothers you about what might or might not have happened all those years ago."

"You can't control what people think." She whirled, gaze fierce. "They're going to say things, give me looks, and you can't arrest them over it."

"I'd like to, if that means anything."

Her expression softened. "It does."

"Then you need to trust me." Would she? She had to!

Nicole's lower lip quivered, but she said nothing.

"We need to talk. Call me. But don't wait too long."

She dipped her head and nodded then got into her car and drove away. They were close to something about this case busting wide open. He could feel it. And yet one wrong decision by anyone involved could compound the tragedy.

THIRTEEN

Don't wait too long. Rich's words haunted Nicole the rest of the day. She'd pick up the phone and then set it down, fear winning the war against conscience. The sky had darkened to a mottled purple by the time Nicole worked up the courage to put the call through.

She shifted from one foot to the other as the phone rang. When she handed Rich the pieced-together letter, would he be compelled to arrest her for some sort of obstruction? And what had he thought about her continued meddling in the case by showing up at the Ellings' house? Surely, he must have deduced that she'd found the yearbook. His questions of Hannah betrayed that he'd laid hands on a copy, as well.

"This is Chief Hendricks." His mellow bass fell easy on her ears.

"Can you stop over?" Her voice resonated sorrow and resolve.

"I'm just leaving the office. I'll be right there."

Rich's SUV pulled up to the nonexistent curb at

the front of the Keller home a few minutes later. Nicole waited on the sidewalk, holding the bag with the letter inside. She motioned for him to stay inside his vehicle then climbed in the passenger side of his unit.

"Might as well get it over with. Here." Nicole handed him the bag.

She twisted a strand of hair around a finger, while he studied the pieced-together scraps of paper.

"Where did you get this?" His gaze skewered her.

She rubbed sweaty palms against jean-clad legs. "Can we drive while we talk?"

His stare remained hard on her for several seconds, then he put the vehicle in gear and sent it up the road. Nicole's heart stuttered. The timbre of his voice and the twitch of a muscle in his jaw betrayed banked anger. They headed out of town.

"Now you need to tell me everything you know," he pronounced.

Anybody who didn't come clean after those words spoken in that tone of voice needed their head examined.

A desperate little laugh left Nicole's lips. "I don't *know* much of anything, but terrible suspicions keep racing through my head. Sometimes I think I might go nuts if I don't get real answers soon."

"I'm with you on getting answers."

Rich headed the vehicle out of town onto township

roads. Gravel crunched beneath the tires as farm-steads flowed past. His silence was expectant.

Nicole exhaled a long breath. "I found the letter yesterday in the missing garbage bag. The bag was stuffed in the backseat of my car. There's no indica-tion who wrote the letter or who it was meant for. If the note didn't belong to my grandmother, I assume it came into her hands somehow, and I suspect she tried to destroy it to protect either the author or the recipient or both."

Nicole didn't say that her grandfather was the likely candidate as recipient, but she didn't have to mention the obvious. The knowledge hung heavily between them.

Rich sent her a narrow-eyed glance. "You should have let the professionals handle the evidence."

"I know, but I didn't. You can arrest me if you want, but I assure you I wore gloves, and I kept the garbage bag and all its contents. You're welcome to the whole mess." She spread her hands. "Who put the garbage bag in my car is a mystery, too."

"Someone wanted the letter found."

"But who would have something to gain from exposing the evidence? Not my grandmother, and certainly not any other person who might have been criminally involved in whatever happened to that baby."

"Someone out there knows what happened and

wants the guilty party punished," Rich said, "but they don't care to come forward."

"They also must have been watching our house that night—maybe other nights, too." Nicole shivered. Could this watcher be dangerous? Dangerous enough to attack her grandmother? Maybe the person was mentally unbalanced. Fern Elling's feral gaze appeared in her mind's eye. "Fern's a good half a bubble off center, and not in a benign way like Hannah. She'd have powerful motive to want her son's killer caught, but I can't understand why she wouldn't simply come forward with whatever she knows."

"Fear?"

"Of who? Her husband's a scary guy, but he's got the same reason to expose the killer as she does."

Rich let out a low hum. "Melody was only a toddler when the kidnapping occurred, and Mason wasn't even a glimmer in her eye. Which leaves—"

"Hannah." Nicole finished his sentence with a laugh. "The idea of that sweet, persecuted little dumpling being dangerous is…well, ludicrous. Unless…"

"Spit it out. Full honesty, remember?"

"My grandmother always warned me about her. I never understood why until I found that yearbook photo of her and Grandpa. But maybe the answer goes beyond jealousy of an old flame. Maybe the warning has substance."

"You mean she's some sort of sociopath?"

"Or maybe Samuel is my grandfather's love child with her." Nicole gulped a shaky breath. "There, I said it."

Rich shook his head. "I've considered that possibility, too, but if so, why would Simon and Fern claim the baby as their own? The Ellings are set on having a male namesake of direct descent. They don't even believe Mason qualifies."

Nicole smacked her palms together. "I can't get around that question, either, but I'd like to donate a DNA sample anyway. I need to know if the child I found was my uncle."

"All right."

"Thank you."

Her chest tightened. What if the test revealed a familial relationship? How would she cope with losing an uncle she never had the chance to meet—possibly at the hands of her grandfather, the child's father? Her stubborn, blind-faith resistance to that idea eroded with each new discovery.

Rich brought the vehicle to a halt at the stop sign before a state highway leading back toward the lights of Ellington. On the other side of the road, pole lamps illuminated a half-full parking lot around a supper club. A sports car peeled out of the driveway onto the tarmac, burning rubber toward town.

Hissing a breath, Rich switched on his bubbles.

"Tighten your seat belt. You're in for a ride. That's Mason Elling's car."

Nicole's back pressed into the seat as Rich hit the gas and flipped on the siren. The car ahead of them sped up, and Rich followed suit.

"Taylor Mead better not be in there with him," Rich growled.

"Who?"

"Dr. Mead's daughter. She's been seeing Mason."

"Good girl fascinated with bad boy?"

"You got it."

Nicole gripped the sides of the bucket seat, while Rich got on the radio and called all available units, sheriff and highway patrol included, to intercept the speeding sports car. A mile sped beneath their tires, then two, and then the city sign whipped past in a blur.

Ahead, a black-and-white sat sideways across the road, lights flashing. The sports car didn't slow down. It jumped the curb onto a grassy verge outside a tire shop, whipped around the blockade and reentered the street. Rich didn't slow down, either. Nicole's teeth snapped together as they hopped the curb. He was already giving commands on the radio for a fresh blockade that would funnel Mason's car onto a dug-up street. The terrain would force the driver to put on the brakes.

"We don't want a high-speed chase all over town,"

Rich spoke into his mic. "I need units coming at him from both side streets and the alleys so he can't turn off. I'll be on his tail. When he reaches the dirt pile the infrastructure crew dug out of that road today, he'll have to stop. A parking-lot fence on one side of the road and a tall hedge on the other should keep him from pulling a repeat of his earlier dodge stunt. And there's an eight-foot pit ahead of him beyond the dirt mound. Watch for him to make a break for it on foot. Mason's not going to give up easily."

He lowered his mic, and Nicole met his glance.

"You okay?" he asked. "I wish I could let you out, but I can't stop."

"Go for it. This fool needs to be caught before he hurts someone."

Rich's teeth flashed white in the dimness. "You're the woman of my dreams!"

A warm flush spread across Nicole's skin. Rich was only using an expression, but she liked the sound of those words way too much. She should be dismayed, but things were happening too fast for her to worry about her giddy reaction now. They turned onto a rough and rutted road. The sports car slowed. Marginally. Then it surged ahead, bouncing and leaping like a spooked deer in hunting season. Sirens wailed. Units converged. The dirt pile loomed in front of them, a good four feet of solid blockade. A cracked slab of dislodged concrete leaned against the mound.

Mason's car sped up, and Nicole's heart seized in her chest. The young man wasn't going to—

"Don't do it, kid!"

Rich's cry merged with Nicole's scream. The sports car shot up the unintended ramp and went airborne. For a breathless second it soared. Then it plummeted, front end first, and disappeared. The screech of tortured metal and crash of bursting glass rent the air above the peal of sirens.

Rich skidded his unit to a halt. They gaped at each other.

"Stay here."

Nicole didn't need Rich's terse command. Whatever lay beyond that dirt pile, she didn't want to see.

"I'm alive. I can't believe I'm alive." Taylor Mead kept repeating those words over and over as she clung to Rich's hand. Light from the open rear of the nearby ambulance spilled over them.

The young woman lay on a gurney with her head and neck immobilized, as well as both her legs, which were clearly broken. A few glass cuts marred her arms and face. Around them, emergency workers went about their tasks. EMTs were assessing Mason Elling on another gurney. He wasn't doing as well as Taylor. Massive head injuries. He hadn't been wearing his seat belt when his car flipped and landed in the pit. They'd have to get a crane to fish out the wreckage.

Rich looked up to see Nicole hovering a few feet away, hugging herself and staring around. He'd take her home as soon as the ambulance left with Mason and Taylor.

The young woman tugged on his hand. "You were right about him. Mason, I mean. I thought I could help him…save him." Tears dripped out the edges of her eyes.

Nicole stepped up and dabbed at the wetness with a tissue she pulled from her pocket. She met Rich's approving gaze, colored and looked away. This woman was a compassionate treasure.

"Shhh," Rich told Taylor. "You don't have to talk now."

"But I do. You need to know. He was drunk, raving about the blankety-blank pigs always trying to arrest him. I kept begging him to stop, but he yelled at me that he couldn't let you get your hands on his car. He said, 'I'm not going to take the rap for them.' But I kept begging, and then he punched me in the face."

Rich's spine stiffened. Was the blood beneath her nose and the puffiness under her left eye from Mason, not the accident? What was Mason's car hiding? The vehicle was going to get the fine-tooth comb. And if Mason wasn't so injured already, Rich would be hard put not to return the treatment he'd given this young woman.

"Oh, my baby!" The shrill cry drew their attention.

Sharla hurried toward them. Rich stepped aside, and the doctor leaned over her daughter, touching her face and weeping. Then she whirled on him.

"What were you thinking? Conducting a high-speed chase in town and with my daughter in the car!"

Nicole stepped back from the gurney. "Rich did all he could to stop the vehicle safely."

Sharla glared at Nicole. "What do you know about it? Do you have a child?"

Nicole jerked as if slapped. Rich went to her.

"I'm going to be okay, Mom," Taylor inserted. "It's my own fault I was in the car with a nutcase."

"Oh, sweetheart, I just…"

The words faded as Rich took Nicole's arm and drew her away from mother and daughter.

"Typical parental reaction," Rich said.

"I know." The words were terse, weighted with sadness.

The situation was awful, but something about what Sharla said to Nicole had turned her face pasty pale.

"Let me drive you home."

"Please." Nicole nodded then she gasped.

Rich followed her gaze. The EMTs had stopped

working over the inert form of Mason Elling. One shook her head, the other pulled a sheet over the young man's face. Rich groaned. The Ellings...the townsfolk...were about to get slammed with a fresh shock.

He and Nicole climbed into his SUV, and he gazed at her stricken profile, but held his peace.

Nicole turned her head toward him. "A situation like this gives me a rare moment of gratitude that Glen and I didn't have children."

"You wanted kids?"

"Passionately!"

As Rich wove slowly through the streets toward her grandmother's house, she told him about finding out that Glen couldn't be a father, his bitterness and distraction, her hope to adopt and then his death.

"I'm honored you told me," Rich said. "If my opinion counts, you'd make a great mom."

She brushed a hand under her eye. "But will I ever get the chance to be one? My empty arms make finding that baby under the rose garden so much harder to take. I can't imagine cutting off the life of an infant. Not treasuring a child as a precious gift."

Rich hummed. "You and I feel the same way about a lot of things—kids, too."

"You've raised your family."

He shook his head. "Karen and I wanted more, but after Katrina was born we found out Karen couldn't get pregnant again. Katrina became the center of our world, sometimes to her chagrin."

Nicole let out a small laugh. "I can't imagine you'd want to start that cycle over again, though. You deserve another chance at happiness with a companion who doesn't expect you to change diapers."

Rich's heart tripped over itself. Was she probing to see if he'd be willing to have another family? Was fatherhood one of her criteria for a new man in her life? Rich mentally slapped himself. Why hadn't he picked up on the issue of children sooner? Of course, she'd assumed he didn't care to go the daddy route again. She'd assumed wrong.

"To tell you the truth, populating my lonely home with rugrats would suit me to a *T.*"

He pulled up outside the Keller house, and she stared at him with a grip on the door handle. "You're kidding. Right?"

Rich crossed his heart and pointed Heavenward.

"I thought…well, it seemed obvious." She spluttered a laugh. "And what would your daughter think of such a thing?"

Rich grinned. "I'd have a hard time keeping her away at college if she had a baby brother or sister to play with at home."

"Oh, dear. Oh, my. I think…I can't…" Nicole sounded like someone had body-slammed the air out of her lungs. "I'd better go. Thanks for the ride."

She burst out of the vehicle, scurried up to the house and disappeared inside without a backward glance.

Rich gaped, stunned. He'd expected to hit a home run with her in the kid department. Instead, she ran like a scalded cat. Women! He shook his head and turned his unit toward the Elling home. Breaking the news about Mason to the town's leading family should distract him big-time from a certain dark-haired female with a heart-shaped face and big brown eyes.

Nicole shut the door behind her and leaned against the panel, eyes closed.

Rich wanted children. He *wanted* children. He wanted *children*.

The realization streamed through Nicole's heart in a nonstop paean. Her head wanted to put the brakes on. Just because Rich welcomed children didn't eliminate the obstacle that he was a *cop*. Yes, a cop who *wanted children!* A cop who made her pulse skip with one sidelong look. And when he smiled? Oh, baby! And that brought her back to children. She could feel that little one snuggled in her arms, so sweet, so soft. And that wonderful newborn smell.

Stop it! Just stop!

Nicole opened her eyes and marched into the living room, where she dropped her purse onto the couch, and then proceeded to the kitchen. She needed a glass of warm milk and a night of halfway decent sleep. Like that was going to happen after this evening's horror. She popped a mug of milk into the microwave and slumped with her back against the edge of the counter. Her heart didn't have a lick of sense where Rich was concerned, but after a little much-needed rest, her head would prevail. She'd make sure of that.

The next day found Rich in the office early, despite his late hours the evening before. As he'd suspected, his duty call on the Ellings had been wrenching and wretched. Melody fell apart and wailed like he'd never heard in his life, and she seemed to blame Simon for Mason's death, hurling terrible words at her father. Fern wept silently and hugged herself. Hannah lurked in the background, chin up, gaze sad, as if resigned to continuous disaster. Predictably, Simon raved against the police department and threatened Rich's job, which was what brought him bright and early to the office, fielding calls from public officials, concerned citizens and reporters.

Simon might be interested to know that, except for a few old Elling cronies, public opinion supported the police department. This community knew Mason was an accident waiting to happen. Folks were relieved the wild child didn't take someone else with him. The young man tried though. He surely did. But Dr. Sharla had already been on the phone to Rich this morning, apologizing for last night's outburst. Taylor was going to be fine. With a pair of broken legs to recover from, she wouldn't be heading off to college in the fall as planned, but her recovery should be complete in time. And maybe she'd gained some hard-won wisdom about relationships. That just left the rose garden baby case, the thefts, the attack on Jan Keller, and the arson on his department's overflowing plate.

Rich brought up his e-mail and spotted a message from the MBCA tech in St. Paul. The subject line said DNA results.

"Hallelujah," Rich muttered under his breath and clicked on the message. He read the comparison from the hairbrush and the infant's bone marrow and let out a low whistle.

"Must be some hot mail there, Chief," a familiar voice spoke from his open doorway.

He looked up to see Nicole smiling at him. The wooden set of her lips indicated the expression was a bit forced.

"I hope you don't mind," she said. "The dispatcher ushered me in."

"Not at all." Rich rose. "What can I do for you?"

"I'd like to get that DNA test over with."

"Oh, right." Amazing how awkward he suddenly felt around her. Last night's talk should have been a breakthrough, but it felt more like two steps back. "Come with me."

He took her in the workroom and swabbed the inside of her cheek. As he packaged the sample, he reached a decision.

"Have a seat." He motioned toward a chair at a small table then he shut the door against intrusion. Settling in a chair opposite Nicole, he wound his fingers together and planted his hands on the tabletop.

Nicole let out a small titter. "I feel like I'm about to be interrogated."

"No, I'm going to tell you a few things about this case. Today I will make a public announcement that DNA evidence supports the assumption we've all been making that the infant's remains are those of Samuel Elling."

Breath hissed between Nicole's teeth. "Then why did you take my DNA sample?"

"Even though the DNA on the hairbrush given to you by Hannah matches the DNA found in the child's bones, that doesn't prove Fern and Simon are the baby's parents."

"Of course!" Nicole massaged between her eyes. "I should have thought of that. Thank you for telling me the results first."

She started to rise, but Rich motioned her to stay, and she subsided into her seat.

"Now I'm going to let you in on a tidbit that a reporter mentioned to me this morning—something my investigation had also uncovered. I need you to know so you will be prepared when the detail is released on the news."

Rich hated the misery and fear on her face. If Samuel was Frank and Hannah's love child, Nicole would have more losses heaped upon her—a murdered uncle and a trusted family heritage destroyed forever. He sent up a silent prayer that a different answer—any other answer—would be revealed.

"Samuel was born at a private sanitarium where Fern, with Hannah as her companion, had spent the entirety of her pregnancy."

Nicole's eyes widened. "Only maybe it wasn't Fern who was pregnant. Maybe it was Hannah."

"The information leaves that possibility open."

Nicole looked down and fidgeted with the purse on her lap. "Believe me, I appreciate all you've done— all you are doing—for me, regardless of how the case turns out." She surged to her feet and rushed from the room, lower lip caught between her teeth.

Rich stomped back to his office. If someone would wipe his heart up off the linoleum, he might feel a little less like dirt for dumping that load on Nicole.

His phone rang again. "What!"

"A little touchy today, are we?" Terry's too-cheerful voice answered.

"Sorry." Rich plopped into his desk chair. "What have you got for me?" He'd sent Terry and Derek over to the impound garage to take Mason's car apart.

"Jackpot! It's a miracle that kid's car didn't blow up. All the makings for a Molotov cocktail were in his trunk, including a jug of gasoline. Looks like we've caught our bomber. Maybe if we shake up Mason's cronies a bit, we'll corral a gang of thieves, too."

"Good work, Terry." Rich's spirits lightened marginally. "Turn Derek loose with the fingerprint kit and see whose sticky fingers we turn up."

Rich cradled the phone and sat back in his swivel chair. If Mason bombed the sewing shop, he'd bet the crime had nothing to do with theft and everything to do with his family's newfound vendetta against the Kellers. Did a bunch of trash talk at his house incite the young man, desperate for the approval of his family, to a rash act? Did Mason also attack Jan in her attic? His slight stature matched the vague description Nicole was able to supply.

But why would Mason have taken that yearbook? How would he even have an inkling about such ancient history? And what had Taylor quoted Mason as saying? He couldn't let his car be searched because he wasn't going to "take the rap." Maybe Mason knew about the incendiary materials in his trunk but didn't put them there. Someone else did. Maybe someone else even used his car to commit the crime. In that case, the real bomber was still out there, squatting like some bloated spider ready to inject more poison into this suffering community.

FOURTEEN

Two days later, Nicole studied herself in the full-length bedroom mirror and straightened the collar of the cream-colored blouse she wore beneath her navy blue pinstriped suit. The last time she'd donned this outfit was for Glen's funeral. Today marked another funeral, one Rich thought she shouldn't attend.

They hadn't spoken much over the last couple of days. He was busy with multiple high-profile investigations, so she shouldn't be disappointed about lack of contact. But she was.

It was thoughtful of him to have called her yesterday about the funeral, even though their conversation had been brief. So foolish that her heart went pitty-pat at the sound of his voice. He'd recommended against her making an appearance at Mason's service. She understood his reason. Enough people believed the worst about the Kellers that she might invite unpleasant backlash by showing her face at an Elling funeral.

"Bring it!" she'd told him on the phone. "Innocent

until proven guilty. Isn't that the credo this country's justice system is supposed to live by?"

Rich sighed. "Unfortunately, the social grapevine doesn't apply the same standard."

"I know it, but I need to show the self-appointed judges that I believe in my family's innocence. Staying away from the funeral would feel as if I were tucking my tail between my legs and admitting guilt. I won't do it. I'm going to hold my chin high and pay my respects."

"I can't say I don't admire your guts." Rich let out his mellow chuckle. "Look for me if things get too hot. I specialize at putting the chill on troublemakers."

"I appreciate that. You're going to be at the funeral, too?"

"Suit, tie and all, but it'll be semiofficial."

"Watching for suspicious behavior?"

"Something like that."

"Won't there be ill feeling from certain quarters about you attending the funeral, also?"

"A badge tends to encourage people to curb their baser instincts. I'll be fine."

"Me, too."

Now, staring at the reflection of her whitewashed face and haunted eyes, Nicole wasn't so sure about her declaration of bravery. "God, please help me," she murmured. What was that verse of scripture

her mother used to quote whenever her father's
department faced public scorn?

Nicole opened her nightstand drawer and pulled
out her Bible. The weight was welcome in her hands.
Once upon a time, she'd thumbed up this copy quite
well. She'd been neglecting this book for longer than
she should have. Flipping through the Psalms, she
stopped on a page with highlighted verses. There it
was in Psalm 31, where she'd marked it years ago.

How great is Your goodness, which You have
stored up for those who fear You, which You
bestow in the sight of men on those who take
refuge in You. In the shelter of Your presence
You hide them from the intrigues of men; in
your dwelling You keep them safe from accus-
ing tongues.

The words washed over her, more energizing than
a jolt of strong coffee, more calming than warm
milk. Fortified, she left the house and headed for
the largest and most prestigious church in town.

Where else would the Ellings attend? Her grandmother belonged to a more intimate congregation up
the road, but Grandma said that every Sunday she
drove past the bigger church, the Ellings' Mercedes
was parked in the lot. But, like Grandma said, church
attendance didn't guarantee the status of one's soul.
For too many people, membership in any given

congregation, big or small, was more about social status or family tradition than real faith in Jesus Christ.

Nicole entered the cavernous narthex where little knots of townspeople chatted in muted voices. As she approached the guest-book table, conversations fell silent then resumed as she passed. No one spoke to her. Ignoring the prickly sensation on the back of her neck, Nicole signed in and deposited her memorial card in the basket provided. She put the pen down and glanced around the room.

Near the coatrack that lined one side of the room, Rich stood in a relaxed posture, scanning the area with a steady gaze. No one seemed eager to associate with him, either. He afforded her a marginal nod and a slight quirk of the lips. Her skin warmed. Honestly, the man looked absolutely amazing in a suit and tie.

She ducked her head and started for the viewal line that passed before the casket on the other side of the narthex. A presence warmed her elbow, and she glanced over to see Darlene smiling at her.

"Good for you, chickadee." She winked.

Several other women, Grandma's particular friends, rallied around them. The knot beneath Nicole's breastbone broke apart, and she grinned. They grinned back.

"How's Jan doing?" one said, nice and loud so heads turned.

"Hanging in there," Nicole answered. "They plan to ease off on the sedatives in a couple of days and see what kind of response they can get from her. Whether she can wiggle her toes. Things like that."

"We'll keep a-prayin'." Darlene nodded.

"Your support is worth more than you can imagine." Nicole's heart expanded, and then she reached the coffin containing Mason Elling, and her blood chilled.

Features relaxed in death, the young man's face reflected peace. An expression he'd rarely worn on earth. Had tidbits of the preaching and teaching in this place lodged in some corner of his heart? Did he grab the truth in that instant before his final foolish choice took his life? Tears welled in Nicole's eyes. She prayed it was so.

Nicole's self-appointed bodyguard swept her on into the sanctuary, where they took seats, and the organ soon swelled with the opening hymn. The congregation rose as the coffin was wheeled in by the mortuary attendants, and family members filed solemnly in its wake. Melody came first, head bowed, shoulders shaking. Then trod in Simon, face a grim mask, with his wife beside him, wringing a handkerchief in her hands and staring ahead, unblinking. The haunted look was more unsettling than Melody's honest grief. Hannah trudged alone behind the rest. Her downcast gaze and steady shuffle hid her emotions from the world.

The service passed mercifully quickly. Funerals hit Nicole harder than most. Yet a nugget of scripture, often-heard but newly heeded, struck her heart. "Comfort one another with the Blessed Hope." She couldn't speak for Mason, or any of the Ellings, but she did know beyond the smallest doubt that her father and her husband lived on in a place of joy. If she grieved, she did so for herself, and only for this split second of earthly existence. She was still here, so there must be a reason—a purpose to fulfill.

Nicole inhaled a long, cleansing breath and released it slowly. The veil of darkness over her spirit began to lift. Problems abounded in her immediate future, but if she didn't cling to God in the midst of them, she might as well be dead for all the use she'd be to her fellow man. It was time to walk on in the precious gift of life the Lord had given.

In her newly buoyed spirit, Nicole walked into the fellowship hall to join in the funeral dinner. Scents of stout black coffee and a tomatoey macaroni hot dish, staples at any Minnesota gathering, teased her nostrils. Nicole stood off a little and looked around for Rich. She didn't see him, but maybe he hadn't reached the fellowship hall yet.

A burly young man with a scowling face planted himself in front of her. "Should be you in that casket, woman. Maybe we could plant you under a rose bush." He snickered. "At least there'd be some justice in the world."

Pulse fluttering, Nicole stepped back before the onslaught, and a wall brought her up short. Judging by a whiff of this guy's breath, he must be one of Mason's drinking buddies who'd fortified himself well for this occasion.

The big goon followed her retreat, sticking his face in hers. "Mason didn't do nothin'. We didn't, either. But now the cops are all over us, acting like we're firebugs and thieves. Hey, I got news for you. Mason's the victim here." His big paws made fists. "He's dead, and you're—"

A large hand fell on the young thug's shoulder and whipped him around.

"Get on home, Brent, and sleep it off."

Rich. Nicole released a pent-up breath and slid sideways against the wall toward an open doorway. It *had* been a mistake to come here. Now Rich was stuck with a situation to handle. Conversations had begun to still and heads to turn as Brent responded in loud belligerence. A hefty, middle-aged woman hustled up, took the young man's arm and tugged him toward the main doors. His mother? Her scolding tone reached Nicole's ears, but not her words.

Nicole fled out the side door into a hallway lit only by diffused sunlight streaming through windows in the rooms on either side. Her presence was hindering Rich's need to mingle and listen and observe. If she could just find a back way out of this building, she'd take herself on home and pack for tomorrow's trip to the hospital. She belonged at her grandmother's bedside.

Her low, spiked heels echoed with every step. She moderated her pace to minimize the click-clack as she peered through one doorway and then another. These were classrooms. Evidently, she'd happened into the Sunday school area. Another sound reached her ears, and she halted, breath bated. Muffled sobs tugged on her feet. She moved to the next door and peeked around the frame.

Fern Elling hunched in a child-size chair weeping into her handkerchief. Waterlogged words brushed past Nicole's ears.

"Accursed…reap the whirlwind… Should have stopped it…God will not be mocked… Broke His commandment… Can't go back…undo… Never should have agreed…" And on and on.

Nicole's skin crawled at the eerie echoes of Goody Hanson's demented cries. Should she interrupt Fern? Let her know she wasn't alone?

"What is going on here?"

At the muted bellow, Nicole nearly jumped out of her shoes. She whirled to find Simon Elling striding up the hall.

"I—It's your wife," Nicole said. "She's in distress."

The man reached the door and peered down his

nose at her. "Of course she's in distress. We just lost *another* family member." He turned on his heel, dismissing her as effectively as a slap on the cheek, and stalked into the room. "Fern, pull yourself together. Our guests are waiting in the fellowship hall to start the meal."

Nicole crept past the door, fighting the shivers. If ever there was a man who could kill, she'd just looked into his eyes. Ahead she spotted an exit sign. Finally! An escape into the outside world. She reached the exit and looked back in time to see Simon and his wife disappear into the fellowship hall. A piece of something white on the dark linoleum caught Nicole's eye. She backtracked to the object.

Fern's handkerchief.

Nicole picked it up between thumb and forefinger and smiled. The damp hanky was a treasure trove of Fern Elling's DNA.

After Brent's mother dragged her grown son away, Rich looked for Nicole in the fellowship hall, but didn't find her. He widened his search and ended up by the glass-paneled front entrance area. Outside, a familiar figure rounded the corner of the building and headed into the parking lot. As usual, she'd taken care of herself. She'd found an alternate exit. Nicole got into her car and drove away. Rich watched her go, hands in his pockets, frustration gnawing his gut.

He could have rushed out and spoken to her, but what would he have said? His instinct was something else again. And inappropriate. He wanted to gather her in his arms and kiss her until she forgot everything else but him.

Rich turned away with a low growl about duty and went back to the funeral dinner. Afterward, he changed into his uniform at home and headed out into the country to interview some of the current owners of what had been Elling property—up until the founding family was forced to sell in order to meet the ransom demand. Could there be some common denominator in these sales that he had missed?

He encountered mostly descendants of the individuals who'd made the original purchases. A few times he hit the jackpot. The direct purchaser was still around, and he got a firsthand account. Everyone's situation was a little different. In some cases, the purchaser had been a small, independent farmer squeezed between the massive holdings of the Elling family. At last, they were able to increase their land ownership and bring in a decent income for their families. Then again, some of the land had been bought by former tenant farmers, glad to be out from under the Elling thumb. Until that moment, the Ellings had wanted exorbitant sums to part with their property. When crisis came, they were only too willing to take a fair price.

"We're honest folks," one oldster stated, as Rich sat with him on his farmhouse porch. "We didn't want to cheat nobody out of what was right, but it sure tickled us tenant farmers silly when we finally got our honest chance."

"In a sense," Rich answered, "the Ellings' misfortune became a liberation day for a lot of people."

The fellow frowned, and his rocker sped up. "We all hoped like everything they'd get that baby back. Nobody wants something bad to happen to a youngster. That's another reason we told Frank we'd pay the going rate for the land, even though he said the Ellings might take less."

Rich sat forward, clasping his hands between his knees. "Frank?"

"Keller. That sharp young man had recently come back to Ellington with his accounting degree. The bank snapped him right up as a loan officer with plans for advancement. Bright career ahead of him, and he fulfilled it all. Started as a teller working part-time in high school, got his education and ended up president. True community servant."

Rich gnawed the inside of his cheek. He'd known Frank Keller had been respected as a civic-minded banker with an honest reputation. But he hadn't realized a young Frank had brokered the farm loans on behalf of the buyers that raised the ransom money. Did this citizen of the year also turn around and collect the ransom to line his own pockets? It looked like he was going to have to subpoena old bank records, as well as Frank's personal financial information. Nicole was going to love that.

Rich rose and stuck out his hand to the wizened, retired farmer. "Thanks for the information."

The elderly man clasped Rich's hand. "Don't know if it shed any light, but happy to help with the investigation. If my opinion amounts to a hill of beans, I don't see Frank as a kidnapper, much less capable of hurting a child. Sure hope you track down the weasel who did."

"Thanks. Me, too." Rich waved and climbed back into his unit.

He took a meandering route on country roads back toward the office, giving himself time to think. Frank and Jan Keller's long-standing good reputations argued against either of them being involved in kidnapping and murder. But every piece of evidence, including Jan Keller's mysterious behavior, insisted that they were up to their necks in the crime. Unfortunately, Rich still wasn't in a position to come to a conclusion about Frank or arrest Jan. He agreed with the district attorney: all they had so far was circumstantial. Even the information he'd gleaned today would go under that heading.

What if the circumstances were misleading? Maybe the truth was something quite different than anything anyone had considered. Could there be a nugget of evidence or information out there that would make the circumstances fall into place, forming a far different picture than what everyone assumed?

If so, he needed to find it soon, or the handwriting was on the wall—Nicole Mattson would shake the dust of Ellington from her feet, and she'd take her grandmother with her if the older woman survived. Neither of them could stay in this town under the dark cloud that swirled around them here. Rich pulled up in front of the station, dreading the report he needed to write casting more suspicion on Frank Keller.

The dispatcher looked up from paperwork on her desk. "Nicole Mattson stopped in with some evidence in a bag. She said it contained Fern Elling's DNA. I put it in the evidence room."

Rich's step quickened on his way to the cubicle, little bigger than a closet, where they locked up small items to be used as evidence. Good for Nicole. Now they were one step closer to determining Samuel Elling's exact parentage. Who knew? They could be all wet in suspecting it was anyone but Simon and his wife. On the counter in the little cubicle he found a paper bag with his name on it. Inside was a plastic bag containing a crumpled white handkerchief.

He held it up and grinned. This was going to be shipped to the crime lab in St. Paul along with the evidence from the trunk of Mason's car that sat in a box on the floor under the counter. Derek had spent meticulous hours trying to locate the shadow of a print on the gas jug and empty Sun Drop bottles to no avail. Maybe an expert would find some other kind of trace evidence. At the very least, a lab technician was going to analyze the gas in the jug that currently provided the slight perfume in this enclosed space. Rich had sent Derek and Terry out collecting gas samples from all the area outlets to be sent in along with the rest of the material. Discovering where the gas for the Molotovs was purchased offered a marginal possibility of a lead on the purchaser.

Rich opened the box that contained the items from Mason's car trunk and surveyed the contents—glass shards in baggies, the gallon milk jug that held gasoline, twisted rags, one of those click-style fire-starters, a long-handled windshield scraper, jumper cables and a tire iron. He'd insisted that everything go in for analysis, not merely the bomb makings. Whoever put the incendiary ingredients into the trunk, whether Mason or not, could have left evidence on other items. Terry had teased Rich about an attack of O.C.D., but something bugged Rich about the normal items. Mason's prints were found on the windshield scraper and the jumper cables, but the tire iron had been wiped as clean as the bomb parts. Why?

Rich donned gloves and then pulled the tire iron out of the box. He examined the object under a magnifying glass. This was the cleanest tire-changing utensil he'd ever seen. Not a trace of grease or a spec of dirt. Whoever cleaned this tool was thorough. However, there was an element that didn't wash off as easily as dirt. An article could look clean, but still test positive. Rich got out the test kit, feeling a little sheepish. Who was he kidding? He was no forensics tech. He'd better not mess up any other type of evidence by conducting this little experiment, but he had one of those porcupine-in-his-gut feelings that wouldn't leave him alone.

A few moments later, Rich stared at the results. His gut was right. Human blood speckled the iron. Someone had used this tool on a person. Was it the same perp who attacked an old lady? Who was the victim of violence this time? More critical still, did they survive the assault?

FIFTEEN

Nicole finished packing a large suitcase for an indefinite stay in the Twin Cities and zipped the bag shut. She parted the curtain on her bedroom window and gazed down into her grandmother's backyard. Evening sunlight had stretched the shadow of the maple tree to twice its length. The yellow crime-scene tape was gone from the remnants of the rose garden, the new piping had been laid to the house and the trench filled in. Still, a great sadness fell over Nicole. A terrible tragedy had been concealed under the beauty of the roses, and suspicion clouded the halls of this home she'd once counted a haven.

The words of that angry young man at the funeral played again in her mind, followed by a rerun of Fern's agonized mutters. If only she could shut those disturbing sounds off, but they kept running through her mind. It might have helped calm her unease if she could have spoken to Rich when she delivered Fern's handkerchief to the station. If nothing else, it would have been fun to see his reaction to her gift.

The house phone shrilled and Nicole jerked. She let the curtains fall back into place and trooped down to the foyer to answer it. Maybe it was Rich calling to thank her. Smiling, Nicole picked up the phone and spoke a greeting.

A raspy breath answered her. "You Kellers better leave town. We don't want your kind here. What happened to Jan could just as easily happen to you."

"Who is this?" Nicole demanded, but the telltale click said the person had hung up.

Electric chills coursed through her body. She didn't recognize the voice, but the venom was unmistakable. Had she just been threatened with violence? A graphic image of a bat swinging for her head appeared in her mind's eye. Heart galloping against her ribs, Nicole slammed the receiver into the cradle and backed away as if the attacker might leap out of the handset.

A sudden ring of the doorbell riveted her to the spot. Blackness edged her vision, but a full breath would not come. A fist pounded on the front door. Then a voice called her name.

Rich!

Tension melted and Nicole staggered for the door. She ripped it open, Rich stepped inside, and then she was wrapped warm and safe in his arms.

"It's okay, honey. Don't worry. We'll figure it out." His hand rubbing her back reinforced the soothing words.

Tiny alarm bells jingled in the back of her mind. What was she doing? She shouldn't let this man hold her. He was bound to uphold the law, and she was bound to uphold her grandmother. Besides, Glen was barely cold in the grave.

Nicole disengaged herself and put a few feet of distance between them. "I—I apologize. You must think I'm insane."

"After what that idiot said to you at the funeral, I don't blame you for being upset. Honestly, I could wring some big mouths' necks sometimes."

Nicole shook her head. "Not that. I just had a phone call."

Concern puckered Rich's face. "About your grandmother? Is she—"

"No, everything's the same there, as far as I know. Someone threatened to hurt me if I don't get out of town."

Rich's gaze turned to steel. "Who?"

Nicole spread her hands. "Whoever it was growled in this raspy voice. I couldn't even tell if the person was male or female."

"That does it. You should leave for the Cities tonight and don't come back until this case is solved."

"That could mean never." Nicole's heart twisted. Would she ever see Rich again?

He stepped forward and grasped her upper arms. "Don't give up hope on me now. Your help with

Fern's DNA and other leads I just ran across might bring us answers."

"I want to believe this nightmare will end." She gazed up into his eyes. "And I know you're doing everything humanly possible."

"Then let's believe together for a little Divine assistance."

Nicole allowed herself a slow nod. "All right. Just don't expect me to drive tonight. These past days have exhausted me. I'll get some sleep then go first thing in the morning."

Rich tapped the end of her nose with a forefinger. "Then you'd better believe I'll have a car outside your door all night."

"But—"

"No argument. I'll let you turn in. I just stopped by to thank you for the handkerchief. Get some rest." Rich opened the door part way then looked back at her. "That's an order." He offered her a lopsided grin that sent her pulse skittering.

She giggled, and the terror that had clutched her a few minutes ago faded like a preposterous nightmare. Closing the door after her visitor, Nicole watched through the window as he trotted to his unit.

What a good man. He'd make a great husband for somebody. A pang smote her at the thought of some nameless, faceless female snuggled in his arms. Turning on her heel, Nicole squashed the tiny green-eyed monster by an act of will. She would *not* be jealous over a man she couldn't let herself love.

As she drew a relaxing, hot bath, a persistent whisper breathed through her soul. She was fooling herself if she thought Rich Hendricks hadn't already laid claim to her heart.

Quite a feat. He'd made Nicole smile, while inside himself he was ready to rip someone's head off. Things were getting way out of hand in this town, and if he had to guess who might be stirring the pot with influence and innuendo, he'd put Simon Elling at the head of the list. That man was a snake of the first order, and it was time Rich had it out with the spiteful old geezer.

A few minutes later, a haggard Melody ushered him into her father's study. "Cop's here to see you," she snarled at her father who slouched in a leather recliner before the cold fireplace. A half-full snifter and a half-empty bottle lay near at hand on the side table.

Simon rose, crocodilian gaze on the intruder to his domain. "Quit pestering us. Haven't you done enough damage to this family?"

"The damage was done long ago, and not by me or anyone outside these walls. Whatever has happened started here."

Simon's gaze popped wide, and his color receded. "What do you mean by that?"

"You're a churchgoing fellow. You know there's a scripture that says God will not be mocked. Folks *are* going to reap what they sow."

The other man paced, hands flexing and fisting. "You're not paid to preach, Hendricks. If you've got proof of something, spit it out."

Rich took a step closer. "I've got a container full of evidence from the trunk of Mason's car that is now headed by special courier for the lab at the Minnesota Bureau of Criminal Apprehension. Before the courier picked it up, I made a discovery. The tire iron found in the trunk has traces of blood on it. Mason's not the likely culprit, because whoever used that iron as a weapon wiped it clean."

Simon took up a belligerent stance in front of the cavernous fireplace. "What are you getting at?"

"Let me finish." Rich lifted a hand. "The blood evidence got me thinking. I took another look at the fingerprint report, and an anomaly jumped out at me. Derek found only Mason's prints on the steering wheel of the vehicle."

"So?" Simon crossed his arms over his narrow chest. "It's his car."

Rich spread his lips in a cold smile. "I happen to know that Taylor Mead drove the vehicle just days ago. Where were her prints? Wiped away, of course. Because someone else drove Mason's car between the time Taylor got behind the wheel and the night of Mason's accident. Someone who had access to the car keys. Someone from this household. The person who really bombed Jan Keller's shop and likely the culprit who struck some poor soul with that tire iron." Rich canted his head and studied the man before him. Simon's face had gone purple. "Did a witness get clobbered, perhaps? An accomplice? The only person who's been missing in Ellington since shortly after the bombing is Ralph Reinert. What did you do with the body, Simon?"

"Are you calling me a murderer?" The senior Elling whirled, tiger quick, and then whipped back around with the fireplace poker.

Rich dodged the swipe, but not fast enough to protect his belt equipment. His radio and cell phone caught the brunt and went flying.

Screaming curses, Simon kept on swinging like a demented ballplayer. The bottle and snifter on the side table crashed into splinters. Rich dived for the man's knees, and took him down flat. Simon's head cracked against the thinly carpeted floor, and he went inert, staring in a daze. Rich flung the poker away then hauled his attacker to his feet. Simon stood swaying, head lowered, while Rich snapped cuffs on him.

"I didn't kill anyone," Simon muttered.

"Says the man who took a swing at a cop with the fireplace poker. You won't 'good old boy' your way out of this one. Even Judge Becker would throw the book at you."

"We'll see about that." Steel returned to the Elling patriarch's voice and stance.

Rich escorted the prisoner out of the man's office and past the amazed gazes of Fern and Melody. Hannah was nowhere to be seen. On the drive to the county jail, Simon kept up a litany of threats and curses. So much for being knocked half silly in his study. Jan Keller wasn't the only person with a hard head in this community. Rich glanced at the fireplace poker he'd deposited in the passenger seat, along with the shattered remains of his radio and cell phone. A chill rippled down his spine. That could have been *his* noggin.

But despite Rich's confident statement, Simon Elling wasn't all wet to spout defiance of his arrest. What had transpired in that study was Rich's word against Simon's. Unless something concrete turned up in the evidence he'd sent to the MBCA or something dramatic shook loose in this case, he might well be hauling this evil old soul to the lockup in vain.

Despite all the fears and upsets of the past days, Nicole fell into deep sleep almost as soon as head and pillow met. Sometime in the night, she surfaced near enough to consciousness to dream. Goody Hanson's wizened face, screeching about lies and breaking the sixth, alternated with Fern Elling's distraught wails about reaping the whirlwind and violating a commandment. Words screeched and growled, images cascaded one on top of another. Harsh breathing melded with the nightmare, growing in volume.

Louder… Louder…

Nicole snapped awake and sat up stiff, lungs sawing for air, heart rattling against her ribs. Her own breathing had awakened her. That and a realization.

She knew what the sixth commandment meant. Or at least where to look it up. What deductions led from that bit of research, time would tell. Nicole grabbed her Bible from the side table. She found the book of Exodus and flipped around until she found what she was looking for in Exodus 20—the list of "Thou Shalt Nots" that was the Ten Commandments. Hopefully, it would be the same as the number Goody and Fern meant.

A few minutes later, she had the list sorted out: "Thou shalt not commit adultery." Adultery? Sure, if Grandpa Frank and Hannah were an item once upon a time, they had committed that sin, but there had been no hint of accusation toward her family in the ravings of either Fern or Goody. The swirl of agony and remorse seemed focused on the Elling family alone. Besides, as Rich had pointed out, a Frank/Hannah liaison would not result in an Elling heir. Why had they claimed Samuel as their own and stuck to that story all these years?

Or maybe there was an explanation. Did Hannah and Fern fool the Elling men? After all, the pair had gone away to a sanitarium during Fern's supposed pregnancy. Nicole's research had shown how difficult it was for an Elling wife to survive in that household unless she produced an heir. Maybe the women engineered the switch to save Fern's marriage—possibly even her life. But how awful for Hannah not to be able to claim her own child!

Nicole had no proof that this is what happened, but the scenario answered a lot of questions, except how the kidnapping went down and who exactly shook that poor baby. Regardless, she needed to tell Rich about her deduction right away. Nicole threw on her robe, donned her slippers and headed downstairs to the phone.

From the foyer, she glanced at the living room wall clock and snorted. A few ticks after midnight. She'd been asleep for barely two hours. If Rich was a night owl, maybe she wouldn't wake him up when she called. Nicole tried his home phone, but he didn't answer. Then she tried his cell, but the call went straight to voice mail. She didn't leave a message. What she had to say was too important. She'd try the station and have them send him over.

"He's headed your way now," the dispatcher told Nicole. "Said something about taking a shift outside your house."

"Excellent."

Nicole went to a front window and peered out. A black-and-white sat on the opposite side of a peaceful street bathed in diffused lighting from poles set at opposite ends of the block. Danger appeared to be a million miles away, but the police presence was comforting. She waited, looking out the window periodically, for Rich's SUV to show up.

Ten minutes passed. Maybe she should go out and see if the deputy would give Rich a holler on the radio. Or maybe she should be patient a little longer. She waited another five minutes, but no SUV. Had something happened to Rich? The trip from the station to her address was five minutes, max.

Nicole tightened the belt on her robe and slipped out her front door. She padded on slippered feet toward the police unit. Scents of a still summer night met her nostrils—dust from the dug-up streets, new-mown grass, blooming flowers. Or was that floral scent wafting out the open window of the squad car? She drew close, and a streetlight revealed a pair of silhouettes in the car. One of those profiles was feminine. The man and woman were fully absorbed with one another, heads close. Were they whispering to one another or kissing? Nicole couldn't quite tell, but one thing was obvious—Terry was entertaining a woman in his car while on duty.

Planting her hands on her hips, Nicole took a few steps closer. "Terry Bender, I'd only half believed the stories about you, but this beats anything. Romancing on the county dime."

Terry's head whipped in her direction, and he gaped at her. A feminine chortle of laughter followed, and his lady friend climbed out the passenger side.

Rich's deputy scowled at Nicole. "You may be cute, but you're the nosiest female I've ever met."

"Actually, this works out fine," said the woman.

Nicole looked toward the familiar voice, and her insides froze. She stared down the barrel of a replica of the small Smith & Wesson handgun sitting uselessly in the drawer of her bedside table.

Melody Elling grinned, her teeth an eerie strip of white under the glow from the corner streetlamp. "We were just debating whether my phone call would be the straw that finally made you go away, or if we needed to take more decisive action. Let's go inside and get your bags. Then we'll take your car. You're about to disappear."

SIXTEEN

Rich finally reached the Keller house forty-five minutes later than he'd intended. What a night! Simon Elling resided in a jail cell, fuming about his lazy lawyer who wouldn't come down to see about bail until morning and the stupid pet judge who chose tonight to be out of town. Getting Simon to cooperate with the intake process had been like trying to nail gelatin to a tree. At least Rich had had the opportunity to replace his radio, if not his cell phone.

But then after he left the station to take over for Terry, Rich ran across a domestic disturbance. A woman and her two small children had been locked out of their house by an angry boyfriend. Rich had driven past the little group standing forlornly on the sidewalk in their pj's and stopped to look into the problem. Before he left the neighborhood, the boyfriend was headed for a male friend's house, and the mother and children were in possession of their home and beds once more. How long before the con-artist of a boyfriend wormed his way back inside? A day or two? People's choices baffled him sometimes.

Rich brought his vehicle to a stop behind Terry's unit and got out. Maybe he'd get some peace and quiet now on guard detail. Terry started his car and rolled ahead, but Rich dashed forward and flagged him down. What was the matter with the guy? It was protocol to give a report before taking off. Did the middle-aged Casanova have a hot midnight date waiting for him? Rich approached his deputy's unit, and Terry rolled down his window a bare inch.

Rich leaned close with a hand on the roof of the car. "All quiet?"

"As a tomb," Terry answered, staring at the road as if he would love to rabbit out of here.

A tangle of odors registered on Rich's nostrils. Sweat of a type he'd learned to associate with nervousness, men's cologne—Terry's brand—and women's perfume. Rich had smelled that exotic scent before.

Grunting as if sucker punched, Rich stood up straight. Now he knew who Terry had been seeing on the sly. What else had that pair been cooking up?

Tumblers clicked into place—Melody's fancy clothes, Terry's itch to oust Rich as chief, the way the equipment thieves knew where to strike and avoid the police. That is, until Rich pulled that Lone Ranger at the implement dealership. Terry was slow to show up at the scene that morning and arrived reeking of cologne. Had he doused himself with his scent to cover Melody's…as well as the smell of gasoline? Terry was the best outfielder on the county law-enforcement team. Had Terry's been the arm that chucked that Molotov at him? Had he and Melody been out here plotting against Nicole? Was she all right? Rich's insides twisted.

His gaze locked with Terry's. Awareness passed between them. "Get out of the car!"

Terry's unit peeled out, burning rubber, and barely missed Rich's toes. Rich got on the radio to the dispatcher. He had to repeat his order twice, but at last she understood that he was serious about the command to put out an APB on Terry's vehicle.

Rich keyed off with the station and raced up to the Keller house. The door was unlocked, which didn't bode well. A quick search of the premises revealed an unmade bed, no packed bags waiting for the morning's departure and a Bible on the nightstand open to the book of Exodus. Outside, Nicole's car was missing from the parking pad. Maybe she'd been unable to sleep and headed for the Cities. But that scenario didn't ring true. Nicole was too conscientious not to let his department know if she was leaving. If she hadn't gone of her own free will, then the departure was under duress. Deadly duress, if his suspicions had foundation.

By taking the bags, Melody and Terry had hoped

to make it look as if Nicole took off of her own voli-
tion and thus avoid a search for her for many hours
or even days. That plan was down the tubes, but
would Rich find Nicole in time to thwart whatever
fate they had in mind for her?

Battling waves of panic, he ran for his vehicle. The
area law-enforcement officer would be looking for
Terry's squad car by now, but Rich knew where he
could go to ask questions about his deputy's female
accomplice—or should he say mastermind. Terry
aspired to be a leader—did well with responsibility when someone else got the ideas and gave the
orders—but he was a born follower. Rich drove up
to the mausoleum on the hill. Hammering on this
particular door was getting old, but he kept it up until
a light came on and the portal opened.

Hannah, clad in a frilly robe, blinked up at him.
A sly smile crept over her face. "Have you finally
figured it out?"

"Where's Melody?"

"Melody?" The woman rocked back on her heels.
"That's not what I meant." Disappointment etched
her tone.

"I don't have time to question you about the true
facts of Samuel's birth, but I'm nine-tenths sure you
were his mother."

Hannah beamed and clapped her hands. "There's
more. Have you got it yet?"

"Right now, I need to find Melody. I believe she has abducted Nicole Mattson."

Hannah's smile crumpled. "Oh, no! They wouldn't!" Her face paled. "But how could they? You've already got Simon locked up. Who else would—"

"Later. If you don't know Melody's hideaway, I need to see Fern."

Hannah shook her head. "Won't do any good. She took her sleeping pills."

"I want to see her *now*." If he put any more heat into his glare, Hannah might have melted on the spot.

She cowered, and he couldn't muster sympathy or remorse—not with Nicole's life on the line. Rich strode after her scurrying figure up the stairs and into a suite with a large sitting area and a pair of side-by-side bedrooms. Hannah led him into the one on the left. She flipped on the lights, but the figure under the covers in the massive bed didn't stir. Rich shook Fern's shoulder and yelled in her ear, but the woman rolled over and burrowed deeper under the covers.

Hannah hovered nearby, wringing her hands. "I told you it was no use. You can't wake her when she's like this. She sometimes sleepwalks, but then she doesn't know what she's saying or doing."

Rich jabbed a finger toward Hannah. "Be here,

ready to talk, when I get back. And Nicole better be fine when I locate her."

He stalked out of the house. Where could Melody have taken Nicole that would be private and out of the way? A snapshot of Nicole by his side as they left the courthouse with plat maps of Elling property appeared before his mind's eye. Rich raced to the station and grabbed the maps from his office. Then he went to the cell block and rousted his prisoner.

"Which one?" He waved the plat drawings at Simon.

The old reprobate flopped back onto his cot uttering specific directions on where Rich could go for eternal warmth.

Frustration feasting on his insides, Rich issued instructions to the dispatcher for all units to continue to watch for Terry's vehicle while casing the Ellings' remaining farm holdings. The process could take hours. Elling property was scattered in small chunks all over the county. Rich's gut said they didn't have that long to hunt.

He located the most remote farmstead on the maps and put the pedal to the metal. If he was wrong, he'd never know what might have been his if he could have kissed Nicole Mattson's lips.

"Why didn't you shoot Rich while you had the chance?" Melody paced back and forth across the wooden barn floor, waving her arms—and the gun that had pointed at Nicole the whole eternal drive out to this isolated farmstead. "People would think whoever grabbed Nicole plugged him. The culprit could be any hothead in town the way my dad has the community stirred up against the Kellers. Nobody would be looking for us."

"Riiiight!" Terry curled his upper lip. "And forensics could match the slug to my police special."

Melody stopped and glared at her accomplice. "All you needed to do was bring the body out here. We could have dumped him in the well with Ralph. All the cops would have found at the scene is blood and missing persons. Hah! You could have led the investigation."

Bound to a post in one of the empty animal pens, Nicole watched with a pounding heart. Ralph Reinert was dead? No doubt the well on this abandoned farmstead was the intended destination for her body, too, with or without Rich as company.

"I'm not a murderer like you are." Terry crossed his arms and sulked. "I didn't sign on for people to get killed. Just a little extra money and Rich gone from *my* job."

Nicole gazed around. The dusty, cavernous space was filled with small equipment waiting for sale on the black market.

"At least I can think on my feet and do whatever's necessary." Melody poked a finger at Terry. "Ralph got what he asked for when he tailed Dad out here and tried to stick his nose in our business. Dad was going to buy him off with a cut, but that bigmouthed busybody would have been the end of the whole operation. I saw what needed to be done and did it, just like always."

Scratchy old-style baler twine wrapped Nicole's wrists. She scrubbed it against the rough post and got only slivers for her trouble. Was there anything she could use on these bindings? Nothing presented itself, not even a nail sticking out of the post. At least the feuding couple wasn't paying any attention to her. Yet.

"We'd better stop grousing," Terry said, "and decide what we're going to do now."

Melody sniffed. "I'm headed for a tropical climate that doesn't have an extradition treaty with the U.S. You can come along or stay for all I care. I've had it with this place and Minnesota winters." She narrowed her eyes at a lineup of snowmobiles. "Too bad we couldn't have gotten rid of this shipment. I could use a little more traveling money."

"You're just going to leave your dad in the lockup?"

"Ellings know how to take care of themselves. We're experts at self-preservation."

"Well, if we're going to run, we don't have to kill Nicole."

Yes! You don't have to kill me. Nicole might have hugged Terry if she wasn't tied up.

"*You* might not have to kill her." Melody turned away from Terry and lifted her gun.

Nicole's thoughts froze, and her knees turned to jelly. Was she about to join her grandpa, and her dad, and Glen? Would that be so terrible? Maybe not, but what about her grandmother? What about Rich? Longing speared through her. Why had she not seen until this moment how much she craved to see what might grow between them? Never mind that he was a cop. She could live with that…if she lived at all. Nicole strained at her bonds, but the cords bit her wrists without giving way.

Melody stalked toward her. "There's another thing we Ellings are good at—retribution. Your grandparents killed my brother and destroyed our family financially. Dad made sure Jan Keller doesn't have a business anymore."

Nicole blinked as she absorbed the statement. Simon Elling bombed the store. The realization hardly surprised her.

Melody reached a spot only a few feet from Nicole. "Now I'm going to make sure her granddaughter never sees another sunrise." Loathing flowed in waves from the gleaming gaze above the black maw of the gun. "If that old bat ever wakes up from the coma I put her in, everything she cared about will be gone."

Nicole gasped. "You hit Grandma? Why were you in the attic? Were you trying to get the yearbook so no one would find out Hannah and my grandfather were high school sweethearts?"

"What are you babbling about?" Lines furrowed Melody's forehead, and the gun lowered a fraction.

"Didn't you take the yearbook because it contained a photo of Hannah and Grandpa Frank at the prom?"

"Why would I care about that?" Melody's arm dipped a little more. "After the cops searched that house, Terry radioed me about some vintage baseball cards in the attic. I took the stupid book because the old biddy hit me with it when I sneaked in to swipe them." She touched her cheek where a bruise lingered. "I figured the book might have DNA evidence on it."

Terry let out a growl. "I told you to wait for an opportune time."

Melody rounded on her partner, gun arm flopping to her side. Nicole's legs quivered beneath a weight of relief—however temporary.

"What could be more opportune than when the home's occupants and the police are downtown?" Melody snarled. "You didn't tell me Jan Keller stayed behind."

"I didn't think I needed to—"

"Never mind! We're wasting precious time." Melody started to turn toward Nicole, the gun rising. "I want to get this over with and—"

"What if Samuel wasn't your brother?" Nicole blurted.

"Now you're spouting nonsense again." But the woman's gaze sparked interest.

Nicole launched into a description of everything she and Rich had discovered and the options they'd considered, including the possibility of a Frank/Hannah liaison. Disregarding her fear-parched throat, she talked about herself donating DNA and turning in the handkerchief with Fern's DNA in order to help discover Samuel's real parents. Terry drew close, muttering things like "interesting" and "Rich didn't share that tidbit," and asking cop-style questions. Nicole appreciated his input. Anything to buy time.

Rich, come find me. But would he figure out where these lowlife's had taken her?

Melody studied Nicole as if she were a bug under glass. "Fascinating but ridiculous," she interrupted Nicole's soliloquy. "Samuel was the precious namesake, all because he got XY chromosomes, and I inherited double X." Bitterness tainted her words.

"But what if it's true?" Nicole protested. "What if Fern and Hannah fooled the family? Rich found out they went away together the entire time Fern was supposedly pregnant, and then came back with a baby boy. Hannah could have been the real mother. What if someone in your family discovered the deception? Do you think the child would have been so precious then? Could someone from your household have killed Samuel and staged the kidnapping?"

Melody stood frozen, gnawing on her lower lip. Then she nodded slowly. "Anyone of us would be quite capable of such a thing." She made the pronouncement as if she was proud of her family's capacity for evil. "But if one of us collected the ransom, what did they do with it? We've been living like paupers for years...until I came up with the scheme to redistribute some of the assets in the area. No, I'm afraid your bid for time is over." The gun swung up.

"No!" Terry shouted and dived for Melody as Nicole drew her body as far as possible behind the meager shelter of the post.

The Smith & Wesson barked, and something tugged the loose sleeve of Nicole's robe. Melody, with Terry on top of her, hit the floor and wrestled for control of the weapon. The gun skittered loose across the boards. Melody thrashed, screaming curses. The woman was strong. Nicole knew that firsthand from when Melody had popped that quilt over her head in Grandma Jan's attic and shoved her to the floor.

Terry clawed for the snap on his police special and got it free, but Melody grabbed the gun from his holster. Another shot rang out, and Terry rolled away from Melody. A red stain spread across his chest.

Melody struggled to her feet, panting, lips flattened

against white teeth in a skull's grin. She lifted the larger weapon with two hands and aimed for Nicole. A shot sounded. Nicole waited for pain and darkness to claim her. But Melody cried out and crumpled to the floor.

Gasping air into constricted lungs, Nicole stared toward a shaft of light that had suddenly appeared in the doorway. Had the Lord come for her? No, that was Rich striding into the barn. Nicole's knees gave way, and she sank as low as her bonds would let her, sobbing.

SEVENTEEN

Rich held Nicole close and trembled almost as badly as she did. The danger was over.

The night was bright with more than the moon and stars. Flashing lights on emergency and law-enforcement vehicles crowded the abandoned farmstead. Personnel ebbed and flowed around them, particularly in and out of the barn and near the covered well. No one asked anything of either of them, and Rich was grateful. Since the crime scene was outside the city limits, the county sheriff had jurisdiction and ran the show.

"You seem to have this habit of saving my life," Nicole spoke into his shoulder the same words she'd uttered over and over again in the past half hour. "Thank you for finding me."

Rich caressed her hair. "Losing you was not an option."

She let out a shaky giggle and lifted her head. "I can't believe I'm shivering like it's cold out here or something."

"You're doing great. You did great in there, too." He nodded his head toward the open barn door.

His heart expanded at the memory of her pitching in alongside him after he untied her from the post and tending to her fallen enemy. Without hesitation, she'd whipped off the belt of her robe and bound it as a tourniquet around Melody's leg where she lay moaning on the floor. The woman would have bled out soon if Nicole hadn't helped her while Rich looked after Terry. Neither of the conspirators might live to see the inside of a courtroom, but that matter was now in the hands of the doctors and God.

Rich heard his name called and turned to see the sheriff approaching.

"I'm going to have one of my deputies get your statements then you should feel free to take the lady home." The man looked at Nicole and touched the bill of his hat.

"Sounds good." Rich nodded.

"I second that," Nicole said.

Twenty minutes later, they were headed toward Ellington.

"Settle back and rest," he told her. "You don't have to entertain me with chitchat."

"Actually, I do." She lit with sober excitement. "I figured out a piece of Goody Hanson's and Fern Elling's hysterical babblings. They were referring to the Biblical sixth commandment prohibiting adultery." A heavy sigh left her lips. "Apparently I'm going to have to accept the idea that my grandfather had an affair with Hannah, but I think Fern and Hannah conspired to make it look like Fern had produced the coveted male Elling namesake."

Rich pursed his lips then nodded. "Makes sense. But then who kidnapped and killed baby Samuel?"

"I will never believe Grandpa Frank would hurt a baby, especially his own. I think it was one of the Ellings. Maybe they found out about the switch."

"Then what happened to the ransom money?"

"Aagh! This is so frustrating." Nicole tugged at her hair. "In rounding up Simon, Melody and Terry, we've solved all the current crimes, but still don't have answers for the cold case."

"I think I know who might."

Rich's gaze collided with Nicole's.

She smiled. "Hannah. Maybe she'll talk now that Simon isn't likely to return home anytime soon."

They reached Ellington city limits, and Rich headed his unit toward the house on the hill.

"Shouldn't we wait until daytime?" Nicole asked. "It's not even 4:00 a.m."

"I doubt Hannah's sleeping. She's probably waiting on pins and needles. I paid her a visit when I was looking for you, and she knows you went missing." Rich glanced at his passenger. "She cares about you, I think."

Maybe he was wrong about Hannah's wakefulness.

The Elling home was dark. They got out of the vehicle, and Rich's skin pebbled in the eerie predawn quiet. Even nature seemed to be holding its breath. For what? Rich shook himself. *Cut it out. Your gut's just nervous after the close call tonight.*

Quite a while of pounding on the front door yielded no answer.

Nicole pulled the edges of her robe tight and looked around. "I'm worried. Even if Hannah was asleep, all the racket you're making should have roused her."

Rich tried the door handle. It was locked. "Let's try around back. Let me get my flashlight from the unit."

He retrieved the light, and side by side, they trod around the massive structure. The lights along the side of the home were also dark, the same in back when they arrived at the garden.

"This is Hannah's favorite place," Nicole said, then called the woman's name. No response.

Rich panned the flashlight's beam over hedgerows and shrubs and bedding plants.

"There!" Nicole grabbed his hand and turned the light back onto a sitting place at the heart of the garden. A thick figure slumped on the bench. "I hope she's only sleeping. That's the way she was when I found her in the garden the first time I came here."

They hurried up the pathway.

"It's Hannah." Rich touched the side of the

woman's neck and located the barest trace of a pulse. "She's not good."

"Ah, no!" Nicole cried and bent toward the ground near Hannah's feet. She came up with a prescription bottle. "And this is why."

Rich snatched the radio off his belt. "I'll call for help."

"Do you have ipecac in your unit's first-aid kit?"

"I think so."

"Good. Until doctors can pump her stomach, Hannah has to be made to purge these pills. I'm going to try to rouse her enough to take the stuff."

"I'll go get it." Rich hustled to his car while talking on the radio. He marveled at Nicole's presence of mind in the midst of crisis. If he didn't love this courageous, caring woman already, he would now.

Fifteen minutes later, the ambulance arrived.

"You're really giving us a workout tonight," one of the paramedics said to Rich.

"I'd rather we all got a good's night's sleep instead."

Rich's heart was so heavy, his mind so overloaded and his body so weary, he wasn't sure how much longer he could function. Nicole must feel worse. Finally, the ambulance raced off with its new cargo, and he was free to take her home. He pulled up outside the Keller house, and she turned toward him.

"Come sit with me on the back deck and enjoy a

cup of coffee while we watch the sunrise." Despite the weariness in her eyes, she sent him a cajoling smile. "I'll make the brew decaf because I want a nice, long nap before I head to the Twin Cities yet today."

Rich chuckled. "You talked me into it. If you can keep your eyes open a little while longer, I can, too."

A shadow stole over her face, and she looked away. Did she have something more to tell him? Rich held his peace until they at last settled side by side on the deck. Nicole sipped from her mug. He followed her gaze toward the paling sky, then to the garbage bin by the alley, and at last to the grave site.

"I thought I'd been tested to my limit in the loss department," she said softly, "but in less than a week my whole life has been turned inside out by secrets and lies."

Her free hand rested on the arm of her chair. Rich covered it with his, but she slipped it away from him and reached into her pocket. She drew out a white envelope.

"I found this under Hannah's bench."

Rich frowned. "You should have given that to me immediately. It's evidence in an attempted suicide case."

A sharp look chided him. "Arrest me later. It's addressed to me." She showed him the handwriting on the outside of the envelope.

Rich sucked in a breath. "It matches the penman-ship on the letter your grandmother tried to destroy. Let's see what's inside."

Nicole opened the envelope, pulled out several sheets of stationery, and began to read aloud.

"'I can no longer live with myself because my long silence has caused harm to Frank's granddaughter.'" Even after only one sentence, Nicole's heart began to flutter. What would this letter reveal about her grandfather? "'A dearer friend no woman ever had, and I have betrayed his memory from selfishness and fear. I write this note in desperate hope that you, dear Nicole, will survive the scheming of this terrible family, but if not, then another will find this, and all will at last know the truth. Such honesty is the least legacy I owe this world that I am leaving.'"

Nicole laid her cup down on the deck table and cleared her throat. "I hope we got to Hannah in time."

"Me, too." Rich nodded. "My prayers are with her and with the medical staff working to save her. But it may be a while before we know for sure."

Nicole returned her attention to the letter. "'Let me begin by assuring you that Frank had nothing to do with Samuel's conception or his de-eath.'" Her voice broke. She squeezed her eyes closed and turned her face Heavenward. "Oh, thank You, God...thank

You, God…thank You, God." The stationery rattled as her hands began to tremble.

Something tugged on the papers, and Nicole opened her eyes to see Rich holding on to a corner. "Do you want me to—"

"Yes." She shoved the letter at him. "I want to know everything, but I don't think I could…read more out loud…" She wiped wetness from her cheeks with her fingers, spluttery laughs escaping her lips. "How could I ever have doubted my grandparents?"

Rich's gaze left hers and fell to the letter.

"'The truth is far darker than the affair your grandmother suspected and hated me for. But neither Frank nor I dared dispel her suspicions. You will soon understand why. I did not know it the day we gaily celebrated Fern and Simon's wedding, but the moment they said "I do" my life was over.

"'The courtship had been a fairytale whirlwind, for Fern at least. In hindsight, I see that Simon scooped my sister up for her social standing and the wealth an orphaned heiress and her underage sister could add to the Elling coffers. Faithfully producing a male heir was assumed. My sister neglected to inform her groom that long-standing female problems had rendered that expectation unlikely at best. Any prospective husband would like to know such a thing before the wedding, but Fern has always been extraordinarily self-centered. Not that I wasn't those many years ago.

"'When the truth came out, the information was beyond devastating to a family such as the Ellings. Divorce was considered, but the disgrace of a failed marriage before the whole community was not on the Elling family radar, especially in that day and time. The summer I graduated high school and shortly before I was to leave that house (eagerly, I might add) for a fine arts college on the East Coast, an alternative plan was hatched. *I* would produce the coveted namesake on Fern's behalf, and my consent was not required.'"

A squeak squeezed out from Nicole's tight throat. She clamped a hand over her mouth. Rich's gaze locked with hers and reflected the horror in Nicole's heart.

She lowered her palm. "How awful for Hannah!" Nicole drew her brows together. "But Samuel wasn't born until Hannah was at least twenty-two years old. Melody came first, which means—"

"Your deduction is correct." Rich's lips thinned. "The next line says, 'The first attempt resulted in a baby girl.'"

"I cannot believe what I'm hearing!" Nicole leaped to her feet and crossed the length of the porch. "That poor woman was subjected to this…this *arrangement* for years! How could her sister sit by and allow it?"

"Hannah makes excuses for her." Rich smacked the paper with the backs of his fingers. "She says that Fern gave in to threats from both Simon and his father, and begged Hannah to cooperate for everyone's sake."

"I can well believe the threats. The Elling wives lived in fear for their lives. But to tolerate this situation for so long and not tell anybody?"

Rich ran his fingers through his hair and shook his head. "People hide all sorts of terrible things for years and years. I see it all the time."

Nicole came back and perched on the edge of her seat.

Rich kept shaking his head. "I'm fighting the urge right now to charge over to the jail and feed a certain prisoner his own false teeth."

"No jury in the country would convict you." Nicole let out a sour snicker, and laid a hand on his knee. "Keep reading. We need to know all of it."

"'A few years later, little Sammy was born,'" Rich went on with the story, "'but there were complications, and I couldn't bear any more children. No matter. The goal was achieved. The Ellings had their namesake, and I could be left in peace. They offered to send me to college, but how could I leave my children, even though I could not claim them? I had hoped to be a positive influence, but as Melody turned out, it's obvious that I failed. Perhaps it's a mercy little Sammy went before he was twisted into the Elling image.

"'You have been patient through this missive to find out what really happened the night baby Samuel disappeared, and now I will tell you. Sammy was a colicky baby and cried a great deal. In the wee hours, I heard him screaming in his crib down the hall. I was so tired, I didn't rise right away to tend to him. His cries abruptly ceased and that alarmed me. I rushed into my son's room to find him in Fern's arms. He was limp. I took him from my sister, but he was already gone.

"'Unseeing, unheeding, Fern turned and left. She was walking in her sleep. As I mentioned to Chief Hendricks this very night, Fern neither knows nor remembers what she does when she walks in her sleep. I am convinced she acted out in her unconscious state the fury she felt toward her husband, toward me and toward the child that wasn't hers.'"

Nicole's grip tightened around the chair arms. If she didn't hang on, she might fly off again. "Hannah is amazing. She's making excuses for that self-centered sister again. What about the kidnapping and ransom scenario? Did the Ellings pull that stunt to avoid a murder trial in the family? Then what did they do with the bogus ransom?"

"Hold on there." Rich held up a palm. "I'm skimming ahead, and it looks like Hannah helped herself to a slice of revenge, and your grandfather aided and abetted."

Nicole sat back, eyes wide. "That helpless-looking dumpling put one over on her abusers? Go on. I can hardly wait to hear."

"'At first, I was so stunned,'" Rich resumed reading, "'I could only stand there with my dead child in my arms. Then I realized I could tell no one in this household what had happened. Even if they believed that Fern had done this in her sleep, they would pretend they didn't and make sure all blame fell on me. I couldn't let them get away with another mockery of justice, another cruelty, so I thought of a plan. Me. All by myself. But I couldn't carry it out alone.

"'My thoughts turned to a friend from high school, someone who had always shown me kindness. I hadn't seen him often after he graduated, only when he was home summers from college and worked part-time as a bank teller. Now he was back with a full-time job as a loan officer—a rising star with his degree, married and poised to start a normal family. Oh, how I envied him. Why I thought it would be a good idea to involve someone like that in a project that could wreck his life, I don't know. But I was desperate, and Frank was one of the few people in town who was unimpressed by the founding family and unafraid of their influence.'"

Nicole clapped her hands together. "Bravo for Grandpa."

Rich chuckled. "The cop in me has to disapprove of what these two did, but the regular guy is cheering."

"Well, get to the punch line, already. Read the rest."

"'I wrapped my Sammy in yard goods from Jan Keller's shop that I'd recently purchased to make myself a dress,'" Rich read on. "'Then I hid his little body in the chest in my room and let the others discover him missing in the morning. During all the fuss, I gave a note to our cook, Goody Hanson, to take to Frank at his place of work. Goody had no idea what was in the sealed envelope, but I'd always had the impression she suspected the truth, and that I had a secret ally. At that moment, I was willing to take a chance that I was right.

"'Goody served Frank and I well as go-between, though we kept her out of the loop when we laid Sammy to rest under Frank's roses in the middle of a fall night and when we collected the ransom. I chose the amount because my innocence was stolen in 1957 when I was eighteen years old—thus $5,718,000. Over time, Frank used his banking expertise to slip every dime of that money to charities as anonymous donations. Hardworking people in the area got the chance to own property at a reasonable price, and the Elling fortune was distributed to the needy.

"'In only one item did we deviate from my original desires. I had wanted to bury my son in the garden behind my house, where I could be near him all the time, but Frank said no. We had a gardener then. Frank feared the remains would be found. At least, if we put Sammy beneath Frank's lawn, the spot would be secure and faithfully tended. I acquiesced, and now I wish I hadn't.

"'Sammy's remains have come to light after all and cast an undeserved shadow over the Keller family. I can only beg you to forgive me, Nicole. I know you will give this letter to the proper authorities, and your family will be exonerated of kidnapping and murder, though some may sit in judgment on the legalities of what we did to serve justice on Simon and his father. Forgive me also for putting that trash bag in your car. In my agitation and eagerness to do what I could to nudge the truth into light, my action made things worse for your family.

"'No one need concern themselves with punishing me. I am punishing myself.

"'Be well, be happy, dear Nicole. I wish the best for your grandmother also. I am not a good person like Frank, so I don't suppose I will see him where I'm going. Don't give me another thought. My time is over. Live out yours to the fullest, and never be afraid, as I was, to speak up for the truth and stand for what is right.'"

Rich folded the letter. "'Signed, Hannah.'"

Nicole hung her head. All the mysteries were solved. All the questions answered. She should be filled with joy that her grandfather would not be known to posterity as a baby killer or an adulterer, though some might judge his collaboration with Hannah. The letter of the law condemned their actions. But what about justice? A bittersweet sorrow enveloped her spirit. Her conservative grandfather was a bigger risk-taker than she'd ever dreamed, and poor, brave Hannah was a far better woman than she knew.

Please, God, let me have the chance to tell her so. And to assure my grandmother that her husband was faithful to her until death.

Without a word, Rich wrapped an arm around Nicole's shoulder, and she welcomed his solid comfort.

Two weeks later, Nicole sat at her grandmother's hospital bedside reading from the Ellington newspaper, heart overflowing with thanksgiving. Grandma had awakened permanently from her coma a few days ago. Her speech might be a bit slurred, her walk halting and her coordination a little off, but physical therapy was already helping bring back function. Tomorrow Grandma could come home, sad about her shop, but willing to try a new business after the reconstruction.

"What was that you just said, dear?" Grandma lifted her bandaged head from the pillow. Her eyes were bright and alert. "I thought you were reading the news report from the last city council meeting, and I could grab a little snooze."

Nicole laughed. "Yeah, this move of the city officials is kind of startling, isn't it? I'll read the paragraph again. 'The city manager reported to the council regarding his research on the procedure to change the town's name. A motion was made and seconded to begin the process. The motion was unanimously carried. City residents will be given an opportunity for input on choosing the new name.' Awesome, yes?" Nicole grinned at her grandmother.

"How low the mighty have fallen when their own town doesn't want their name." Grandma tsk-tsked. "Is there any more in that paper about the town heroes?"

"Who?"

Grandma sniffed. "You and Rich, of course."

"Oh, Grandma!"

"Don't deny it, young lady. You survived abduction and a murder attempt. That Melody and her accomplice, Terry, are headed for long stints in prison, along with that no-good Simon. And, to top it off, you and that handsome police chief of yours solved a half-century-old kidnapping and murder case."

"Rich is not *my* handsome police chief."

"Ah-ha! You admit he's good looking." Grandma wagged a finger at Nicole. "I think he's sweet on you."

Nicole scrubbed a hand over her face. "Grandma, nobody says 'sweet on' anymore."

"Semantics, shamantics." Nicole's grandmother sniffed. "Have you finally realized you were born to be a cop's wife?"

Nicole's face warmed. "It's a little premature to be planning a wedding."

"Who's planning a wedding?" Rich's voice came from the doorway.

Nicole turned his direction, skin flaming. "Grandma's indulging in idle speculation."

"Nothing idle about it." The older woman chuckled. "Grandmothers know these things."

Rich laughed and brought his arm from behind his back. An abundance of roses filled his hand.

"What a lovely bouquet," Grandma said.

"Two bouquets. One for you." Rich stepped into the room and placed an arrangement on the overbed table by Grandma's bed then turned and extended the other bouquet toward Nicole.

Pulse skipping, she took the offering and smelled the fragrance of the yellow roses, so like her grandfather's favorites from his garden.

"Told you he likes you." Her grandmother chortled.

"Thank you," Nicole told Rich. "I like you, too. Just a little." She quirked a small smile.

He grinned that scrumptious grin of his, and

Nicole's insides did twirls. "That's a good start," he said.

"Given a little time," Nicole said primly, "I might decide that receiving flowers from you should become a tradition."

"Since crime in Ellington has been reduced to jaywalking, I've got plenty of time on my hands." He winked at her.

Everyone laughed.

Nicole sobered. "I'm so glad Hannah survived. How is she doing?"

Rich's grin faded. "She spent three days under evaluation in a mental-health facility, but they gave her the green light to be released into outpatient care, poodle skirt and all. Her sister, Fern, didn't fare so well. She lost it completely when she found out the last of the Ellings were going to prison. No one's even told her yet that she killed Samuel. Somewhere deep inside, I suspect she knows. She's been committed indefinitely, which is a measure of justice. There isn't enough hard evidence to take to a murder trial, even though DNA testing has confirmed Samuel's proper parentage. Hannah's now the sole occupant of the house on the hill."

"That poor woman," Grandma Jan said. "What consequences will she face for that fake kidnapping scam on the Ellings?"

"None." Rich spread his hands. "The statute of limitations expired on the offense long ago."

Nicole looked from Rich to her grandmother. Why did Grandma look so troubled? "You think she should be punished?"

"I'm the one who deserves consequences." Grandma slowly shook her head. "Decades back, I found that letter from Hannah to my husband and leaped to a conclusion without talking to a soul. I thought I was being noble to quietly forgive my husband and move on with our lives. The truth is I was embarrassed. Humiliated. It was easier to sweep the matter under the rug and bear a grudge against Hannah. That was wrong. May God forgive me."

Nicole grasped her grandmother's hand. "He has, you know."

"I know. But when I get back on my feet, I'm going over to see Hannah. Someone needs to tell that dear lady about the grace and mercy that's available to her, too."

"I'll help you with that."

"Count me in," Rich said, stepping forward.

Smiling, Nicole took his hand. Her fingers felt so right in his. Rich grasped her grandmother's other hand. Deep peace spread warmth through Nicole's insides. Their little ring of faith felt like a true family—a place of belonging, safety and hope.

EPILOGUE

Five Months Later

Nicole scooped up twin handfuls of snow in her grandmother's backyard and molded the wet mounds into a single tight ball. "Hey, sweetie!" she called.

Rich turned from positioning the carrot nose in the snowman they'd been putting together this bright Saturday afternoon early in December. Snorting a laugh, Nicole fired her missile. The snowball splatted on the front of his jacket. Roaring, Rich charged for Nicole. She whirled with a shriek and ran, but not fast enough. A big body knocked her flat into the snow. Chill crystals sprayed into her face. Her high shrieks of laughter mingled with his rumbled chuckles as they wrestled. Rich came out on top, and she let him steal a kiss. Then he rolled away, still laughing. They lay on their backs next to each other, puffing out smoky breaths.

"Good thing your grandmother is Christmas shopping with her friends," Rich said, "or she'd be standing on the deck scolding us for acting like kids."

"Right before she chucked a snowball at us." Nicole giggled. "Can you see that crew of hers? A half dozen spry little old ladies swooping through the mall. Darlene stomping around with her cane, marshaling the troops like a general. Grandma making lists and checking things off. And Hannah—"

"Now there's the biggest surprise. Nowadays, she looks like the most normal in the bunch."

"She likes jeans and T-shirts almost as much as I do." Nicole pursed her lips. "Sometimes I kind of miss her crinolines and dancing slippers."

"I can't say I do. I'm glad she gave herself permission to join us in the twenty-first century."

Nicole rolled onto her side and mentally admired the handsome galoot sprawled beside her. These months of getting to know one another since solving the crime of last century had been so precious. "Laying her little Sammy to rest in a proper burial spot was the best therapy she could have received."

"No arguments there." Rich rose, grunting.

Nicole took his outstretched glove and let him help her to her feet. They dusted snow off themselves.

"Let's finish Mr. Snowman," Nicole said.

They returned to shaping and patting, chattering lightly about their day. Nicole was abuzz about the orders streaming into the shop. "And Grandma is having no end of fun designing new logos. I don't even have to tell her 'I told you so.' She says so herself every day."

"What an awesome God we serve." Rich grinned. "How things have turned around so quickly. You might be interested to know that the accountants and attorneys have wrapped up the combined IRS-law-enforcement investigation into the Elling finances. That bunch has been lying, cheating and stealing for years, just to keep their heads above water in that mausoleum of theirs."

"The authorities are going to release Hannah's money then?" Nicole's heart leaped.

"That's right. Major Christmas present for her."

Nicole smoothed the snowman's plump belly. Earlier in the investigation, a hidden trust fund had been uncovered with Hannah's name on it—a substantial sum set aside by her parents before their deaths. She'd been well off since she was a teenager and hadn't known it. Another kindness for which she could thank her sister, Fern, the executor of her parents' will. It must have grated the Ellings every minute of every day that they couldn't get their hands on all that money moldering in the bank.

"What is that evil grin about?" Rich asked as he fit a stick arm into one side of the snowman's body.

"I'm always tickled when the underdog gets the last laugh." Nicole wrapped a knitted scarf around the snowman's neck. "Now what shall we name this guy? Mr. Snowman doesn't quite cut it."

"How about Parson Brown?"

Nicole stared up at Rich. The intensity of his gaze warmed Nicole's skin. "Parson Brown? I don't know any pastors in the area by that na— Oh, you mean like in the song, 'Winter Wonderland'?"

"You catch on quickly." His gloved hand dipped into his jacket and came out holding a square box. He held it toward Nicole.

Big-eyed and breathless, she stared down at the plump box covered in blue velvet. "Is that—" She halted on a dry mouth then licked her lips and swallowed. "Is that what I think it is?"

Rich flipped it open. A diamond on a gold band glittered back at her. "I love you, Nicole Mattson. I was hoping later on this evening we could conspire by the fire. Make some 'I do' plans."

Pulse thundering in her ears, Nicole averted her eyes from the hot hope in his. Finger by finger, she pulled off her glove. Her bare hand trembled as she held it toward him.

Rich tucked his hand under his arm and pulled it free of his glove. His fingers were warm and gentle as he slipped the ring on her finger then clasped her hand in his.

Nicole lifted her head, lips parted. His mouth lowered to hers, and she received the kiss with all her heart.

* * * * *

Dear Reader,

Nicole and Rich survived deadly trials with their faith strengthened, their hope renewed and their hearts bound in love. They faced difficult, even shocking, issues that made them appreciate the blessings of life and family more deeply. Nicole realized that protecting her heart was more costly than risking it. Rich ran across the biggest case in his career and discovered how far short man's law can fall in providing justice for the innocent.

I want to thank Sherry Deyo, RN/PHN, for providing health-care information. Deep appreciation goes to the Steeple Hill staff for all the wonderful things they do to bring these exciting tales of faith and hope into your hands, dear reader. I particularly want to thank my savvy editor, Emily Rodmell, for her fabulous insights that enrich the story. I also need to say to my family, especially my husband, thank you so much for your love and support (and your patience when I am wrapped up in deadline). I couldn't write without you, dear fam!

And without you, dear reader, stories would have nowhere to go. I invite you to visit me on the Web at www.jillelizabethnelson.com. Read on, faithful ones!

Abundant Blessings,

Jill Elizabeth Nelson

QUESTIONS FOR DISCUSSION

1. Nicole and her grandmother have different visions for the same business. Clashing visions happen in relationships. How do you resolve these important differences in a Godly fashion?

2. In times of grief, we seek safe havens. After losing her husband, Nicole returns to a person and a place that has always equaled security to her, and then a shocking discovery threatens everything she trusted. How does she react? How would you react in such a situation?

3. Rich has been admiring Nicole from afar with plans to kindle a romance. The resurrection of this cold case brings Rich's duty into conflict with his heart. What is more important, heart or responsibility? Can the two be reconciled? Why or why not?

4. The Elling family has ruled the area with money, influence and outright threats when necessary. These mini-dynasties pervade society. What influence do those in such positions of power have on the dynamics of a community? How does a person of integrity wisely respond to this type of undue influence?

5. Rich's deputy thinks he should have Rich's job. Rivalry and jealousy in the workplace are common. Discuss situations you've encountered or observed. How should these matters be handled?

6. Loss upon loss has been piled upon Nicole's life, and grief has dulled her relationship with God. Where in the story do you see her renew her commitment toward the Lord and why?

7. Why does Nicole become irritated whenever Rich compliments her coplike deductive and investigative abilities? Do you have hot-button issues in your life? Does your touchy reaction indicate a need to look for the underlying cause, and then to deal with it?

8. In her prior marriage, Nicole encountered an issue with infertility. She was willing to adopt a child. But when she lost her first husband and Rich came into her life, she was not willing to consider forgoing children in order to have him. Was this a legitimate concern or an excuse to protect her heart? How about her decision never to marry another cop—legitimate concern or excuse? Do we often set up criteria in our relationships that are designed to protect ourselves?

When is this a good thing and when does it have negative effects?

9. Despite the Keller family's long-standing respect in the community, people's opinion turns sharply against them after the infant's remains are found. Have you encountered similar rushes to judgment? What position should a Christian take when circumstances arouse suspicion but not all the facts are in?

10. Nicole saw the devastating results on her family due to reporting her discovery of the remains at the beginning of the book. Later in the story, she encounters another piece of important evidence, but she hesitates to report it to Rich. Are her reasons compelling?

11. Mason is a bad boy who wreaks havoc wherever he goes and nearly gets an innocent young woman killed. He's also suffered rejection by his family from the day of his birth. Does his pain excuse his behavior? Why do bad boys fascinate good girls—or vice versa?

12. Hannah's psyche becomes stuck in the '50s. Why? And why might she continue to make up excuses for Fern no matter what her sister does?

13. What is the basic fear behind the Ellings' obsession with carrying on their name? What goal do they expect to achieve by perpetuating their lineage at all costs? Is this thinking rational?

14. Discuss the affect of this tragic obsession on the following characters: the Elling patriarchs (Seth, Silas and Simon); the Elling wives, including Margaret and Fern; Melody and Mason; Hannah; Frank and Jan Keller; Nicole; the community of Ellington. Could every one of them be considered a victim in some way? Do they all commit or omit something that allows the obsession to continue? Who would you name as the truest victim in this story? Why?

15. Discuss Frank and Hannah's response to Elling evil and the death of baby Samuel. Were they justified in their actions? What might you have done if you were Hannah or Frank?

LARGER-PRINT BOOKS!

**GET 2 FREE
LARGER-PRINT NOVELS
PLUS 2 FREE
MYSTERY GIFTS**

Love Inspired

SUSPENSE

RIVETING INSPIRATIONAL ROMANCE

Larger-print novels are now available...

LISUSLP10R

Love Inspired.
HISTORICAL
INSPIRATIONAL HISTORICAL ROMANCE

Engaging stories of romance,
adventure and faith,
these novels are set in
various historical periods
from biblical times
to World War II.

NOW AVAILABLE!

**Steeple
Hill®**

For exciting stories that reflect traditional values,
visit:
www.SteepleHill.com